Uncommon Magic

Fairy Tales
For Grown-Ups

By Tyger Schonholzer

Cover Art
By Michaela Jayde Richardson

All Rights Reserved

This is a work of fiction. All characters and situations are figments of my imagination. Any resemblance to persons living or dead are purely coincidental with exception of the story 'The Kiss That Changed The World,' where the character is real but the story completely made up.

ISBN-13: 978-0692493946

ISBN-10: 0692493948

Dedication and Acknowledgements

This book is dedicated to my mother, Annemarie Schönholzer, who taught me to write, and whose encouragement helped me believe in myself. She did not live to see this book published, but she read many of the stories in their draft stage. I will always be grateful for her advice and inspiration.

My gratitude also to my friends at the Deskdrawer and its creator Michelle Hakala for many valuable ideas and helpful critiques. My thanks also to Murielle Hamilton for inspiring 'The Veils,' to Vicki Bond who prompted 'The Shoe Princess,' and to Taichung Allen, whose interest in mermaids kindled 'Cold Maid.'

Lastly, my appreciation and love go to my family and close friends for their patience and support.

The story 'Nightingale' was previously published by *Fictionvortex* and 'Favorite Meal' was previously published by *Bewildering Stories*

Table Of Contents

The Indistinct

Dementia is a human plague, so why am I displaying symptoms of their dreadful disease? Here I am, trapped in a jail cell like an imbecile. I am doomed. Who ever heard of a sprite who forgets how to vaporize?

My story is all about love and hunger, and it began long ago, when I first learned how to walk the earth in solid form. Transformation burns much of our energy when we become flesh, and so I was famished and in search of nourishment. Not sure what would best become my new shape, I picked up various objects and tasted them, only to spit them out again and shudder with loathing.

"By all the gods, you startled me!"

I jumped. My new, heavy body did not levitate sufficiently. To my consternation, I crashed to the forest floor.

"My humble apologies," I stammered, trying to regain my feet. Despite my embarrassment, I did not forget my good manners.

She was human, I knew the instant I caught her scent. She was what I had come here to find, to still my curiosity.

"Oh my…" she said, when I finally managed to rise. Her eyes widened, and a smile graced her lips. "Where are your clothes?"

"I…I haven't any." I had not thought of that. Nudity is not an issue when you're pure energy.

A gentle hue of red crept up her neck and flushed her cheeks, but she did not move or avert her eyes. "Have you come here to harm me then or take advantage of me?"

Had I? I wasn't sure, but it wouldn't do to admit it.

"Nothing would be farther from my mind," I said.

She must have found me pleasing to look at, because she did not run or glance away. I dared take a step toward her but I didn't reach for her. I could sense the warmth from her body, and her scent stirred a longing in me that would trouble me for eons in its ambiguity. Despite my appearance, I was not human, and the aroma which assailed my nostrils wakened my need to mate, yet at the same time I also unmistakably recognized her as food.

"I live not far from here. If you promise not to hurt me, I may be able to give you something to cover yourself."

"By the light and heat of my soul, I promise."

She looked at me strangely, and it occurred to me that such an oath would be foreign to her species.

I followed her gladly. My eyes rested on the gentle sway of her back, where a wealth of chestnut hair cascaded down in soft waves. Ample hips curved generously below a slender waist. Rounded and shapely, bare arms swung by her sides.

"Wait here," she said, when we reached the edge of the forest. "It wouldn't do for someone to see you like this."

Before us, a valley spread with lush fields, interspersed with squat cottages and gardens, brimming with blooms and greenery. She hurried toward one of the cottages, while I hid in the shadows. Humans worked in the fields and in some of the gardens and straightened to greet her when she passed by. I felt trapped at the edge of the wood and for a while feared that she would not return. I relaxed when I saw her reappear with a basket. She took her time coming back and stopped here or there to speak to one of the villagers. When she finally returned to me, I fidgeted with impatience.

She laughed. "I told them I would gather mushrooms for supper. And I will, if you'll help me." She handed me a bundle of clothing. "These belonged to my husband. He passed away last winter. You are most welcome to them."

"Husband?" My confusion amused her.

"My mate. You are not from around here, are you?"

"Not in any way that would make sense to you."

Realization dawned on her. "You're a creature of myth? A fawn maybe?"

I picked up my foot to show her that I had no hoofs but soft soles. "Not a fawn, but something like it."

She blushed again. "From what I remember from my husband, you seem to be much of a man though."

"You noticed. That pleases me."

"Can you…are you able to…" she faltered.

"One would assume, but it is something yet to be discovered."

She helped me dress. Her nearness excited me, and, encouraged by her smile, I ran my hands over her arms and gripped her wrists. I could hear her breath catch in her throat.

"Kiss me," she said.

I shook my head. "I don't know how."

She stepped into my embrace and pressed her lips against mine. The fire I felt in my belly, combined with my lack of nourishment, nearly made me faint.

She steadied me and with a worried look asked, "Are you ill?"

"No, but I lack food. I have not eaten since…since…" I could not tell her that, only minutes ago, I was still a flicker of light - pure energy in accelerated motion.

"Oh…what do you…what does your kind eat?"

I avoided her eyes. "I'm not sure, actually, but I think it involves flesh."

As chance would have it, her sideways step stirred up a fat rabbit, and, quick as lightning, she drew a knife and felled the beast with a single toss.

"Help me build a fire and roast it," she said.

I still didn't look at her. "I'd prefer it as it is."

She shuddered. After a moment's silence, she motioned toward the dead animal. "Help yourself."

I was thankful that she didn't watch while I devoured the rabbit. Even to me, a sprite, it seemed barbaric, how I tore at the ears with my teeth, gouged the tender parts from the body and dropped the entrails to the ground, while blood and grime drizzled over my chin and hands.

"You can wash at the brook a little up the path here," she said after I finished, and led the way. Once again, I watched her from behind, committed to memory how she moved, her hips swaying ever so slightly, while her bare feet padded silently on the pine needles.

I felt shy, even after I had washed, but I desired a repeat of the kiss. I stepped toward her, arms wide. "I'm stronger now."

Yet, she backed away. "Mushrooms first," she said and pointed toward the ground, where scores of soft, brown lumps huddled around tree trunks. I picked one up to taste it and spat it out.

She laughed. "We have to cook them first. Now, start picking!"

I had not lost all of my speed and agility, even in this awkward body. I hoped to impress her and filled her basket quickly, taking care to choose only the smoothest, roundest specimens, as I had seen her do. She nodded and smiled. Under lowered lashes, I watched her, and my soul sparkled.

All eyes followed us when we walked side by side through the village. There was a spring in her step, and she seemed to carry herself just a little straighter, hold her head a mite higher than before.

She lived in a small, two-room cottage. Still not used to the feel of solid matter, I explored the thick, braided rug with my bare feet and ran my hands over the sparse, but sturdily crafted wood furniture.

"Do you like it? I made it myself and painted the cabinets, although my husband built the house."

I nodded. The flowers, painted on the cabinet doors, looked almost real. If a breeze had touched them, they would surely have moved. On her wall hung a likeness of her and of a human male. I stared.

"My husband." Her eyes moistened with wistful pensiveness for a moment.

I hated him on sight. The intensity of the emotion caught me by surprise. I wanted to take her in my arms and kiss her again. I wanted to cover her, ravish her body and blot out all memory of him for ever. Was this what it was like to be of the flesh?

She washed the mushrooms in a pail of water by the stove. Quickly and expertly, she lit a fire and warmed butter with chopped herbs in a skillet. She fried the mushrooms and cut up and added some starchy red tubers. The smell from the tubers was questionable and made me sneeze. Finally, she took from a cabinet a hunk of smoked flesh, still on the bone, cut fine slices and dropped them in the pan. That improved the odor somewhat.

She placed two earthenware bowls on the table, ladled the food into them and bade me sit down and eat. I did not think the tubers would agree with me, but I wanted to please her, so I resolved to eat them anyway.

Just as we dipped spoons into the hot meal, a knock at the door stirred her from her seat. She only half opened the door, but I could see several faces staring in at me. That raised my ire.

"I have company," she said. "Come back tomorrow."

I heard the sharp intake of breath. "Scandalous!" said a voice. "He hasn't been in the ground six months yet."

Her head dropped, and she shuffled her feet. Even I felt her embarrassment. I wanted to help her. I took the door from her and placed a hand on her shoulder.

"She cooked mushrooms," I said, "and she did not invite you. While I understand that this upsets you, I assure you, there are plenty more out there if you wish to pick your own."

She cried out then and moved away from my hand. Fine mists of smoke rose from her shoulder, and a hand print darkened the fabric

12

of her dress. I slammed the door and rushed to comfort her.

"That felt like fire! What are you?"

"I am so sorry. I had no idea this would happen."

I reached for her, but she withdrew. "Don't touch me!"

I willed myself to calm and held out my hand. "I won't hurt you now, I promise."

She hesitated, but then took my hand. "Why did you burn me?"

"They angered me and must have roused the fire in my soul. I did not mean to hurt you with it."

"They are just villagers. They have done nothing to you."

"They stared. In my world it is rude, even dangerous to stare." Two sprites staring at each other could cause an explosion. But how to explain this to her? "Besides, they caused you distress. I cannot allow that."

She threw her head back, and her chestnut mane whipped around her shoulders. "It is not your place to allow anything. I am a free woman. You are not the master of me!"

She let go, and my arms fell to my sides. I felt as though I had been struck or dowsed with cold water. When my elders disciplined me, I had felt so wounded. The light inside me dimmed, and I stepped back. I might have left then, had I been less captivated. Something in her eyes held me fast, and I stood meekly, like a beggar before her.

"I meant only to help…by the custom of my kind."

"I see," she said more gently. "Understand, that by the custom of *my* people, you have offended me. A man may only step in, if a woman asks for help."

"What a strange custom! What if she sleeps and cannot ask?"

She smiled and when she did, my soul lit up again. At once, I moved forward and took her into my arms. I kissed her, and I fell into that kiss as one falls into the Sea-of-Fire and it felt just as sweet.

"I have never mated with a human. Show me what to do."

It was painful, yet blissful to follow her guidance. I had to hold back my fire, so I would not injure her yet give her enough heat to please her. In the excitement, I bit her lip, bit deeply and tasted the sweetness of her flesh. Oh what ecstasy to mix food and pleasure!

She pushed me back and planted her fist in my ribs. When I urged forward again, her hands found my throat and tightened around it. Her piercing scream would carry far, and I thought to quiet her, but I had not the breath to do it. I pinned her arms down, but then, despite the struggle, she climaxed and relaxed under me. I fell upon her throat and poised to bite, when her voice stopped me.

"Don't! You are hurting me."

When release came, I did my best to control my fire, but I still singed her. She crawled from under me and ran to the water bucket to dowse her angry red skin. Her dress lay crumpled on the floor, and she grasped it to cover herself.

"What *are* you?"

When I didn't answer, she dropped the dress and dowsed me with water. I leapt to my feet and stood, breathing heavily.

"You tried to eat me! Are you a monster?"

The look on her face stung me. Terror and disgust overshadowed her lovely features.

I shook my head and stared at the floor. "I don't really know what I am now."

She stared, trembling. I was still unclothed, and after a while, her gaze softened, and she reached out for me.

"You look like a man, and you feel like one, but you don't love like a man."

"I'm so sorry." I could only whisper. I had felt shame before, as a sprite, but now that I was flesh, it stung so much worse. Despite her scorn, I still desired her, and despite her earthy beauty, I still hungered.

"I had better leave now. I have caused you too much grief."

I waited, but she didn't answer, so I moved toward the door.

"Wait! You may keep the clothes."

I shook my head. "I won't need them where I'm going."

She hugged herself. Her breasts swelled above her crossed arms like ripened fruit. I longed to touch them, to rub their velvety softness against my cheek, my lips, my tongue. I felt passion rise again, and she saw it.

"Go now, before the sun falls, so you can find your way. Take the clothes, so the villagers won't harass you." And in a quieter voice, she added. "...and keep them, in case you ever wish to come back."

I would not, I resolved. When I walked out of her door that day, dressed in human garments, I was certain I would never see her again. How little did I know of the ways of the flesh!

I'm not sure what made me hide the garments in a place where only I would find them again, but I was naked when I vaporized, and only the flesh and bone burned up in the transformation and fell to the ground as ash.

A fine mist hovered over the site, where the body's moisture had turned to steam. I saw it in the moment of transformation, before I gained speed, and then it winked out of existence, and I was home.

I dove into the Sea-of-Fire and reveled in its bliss for an eon, before I emerged to flicker in the night. I noticed right away that something had changed. Although, I had not lost velocity, I now felt a subtle *spiritual* slowing down, as if my soul had become hesitant in following its inner light.

And of course, I could not forget her.

Time and again, I was drawn to the coordinates, where I knew her house stood. I found myself there without aiming, yet I somehow felt her when I hovered there. I wished I could have visited her in my sprite form, to spy on her in the night, when she was sleeping, but I could not decelerate enough to see her.

After yet another eon, I gave in to the craving and re-entered her world. It was still summer – or maybe summer again – and the villagers scrambled through the fields, bearing rakes and pitchforks and pulling wagon-loads of grains and tubers. They stopped to gawk, but I willed myself to ignore them.

She stood by the stove. A familiar smell of wild mushrooms and herbs drifted toward the open door, and I smiled. Was she expecting me?

"I would have helped you gather them, had I known you would cook for me."

With a cry, she dropped the spoon and whipped around. Both hands flew to her face. She blanched and looked as if she would faint. I feasted my eyes on her.

"By all the gods…!" she cried.

And then she did faint. I caught her as she went down and carried her to the cot, where I lay with her until she stirred again. I held back my hunger and only warmed her gently with my fire. That was the moment, when time should have stopped passing, and nothing could have marred my joy.

"Get the bloody hell away from my wife!"

Rough hands gripped my shoulders, and to my shock, I was ripped from the cot and thrown into the far corner of the cottage. I fell against the wall with a thud and slid to the floor. Had I fallen any harder, I would have heard bones crack. So unexpected came the attack that I felt many heart beats pass before I caught a breath. My assailant did not wait that long, but fell on me with ferocity. I had never fought a human, and I suffered several blows before I caught on to his style and managed to guard myself.

I faced a tall, stocky man with powerful arms and hands, hardened from daily labor. His dark scowl frightened me as much as his mercilessly pummeling fists. He outweighed me by at least fifty pounds if not a hundred. He would have killed me, if she had not stepped in.

She leapt into his arms and held him back. "Don't hurt him! It is not his fault. He doesn't know!"

He backed away then, and she rushed to my side. "Are you injured?"

I shook my head and searched her eyes for answers. "Who is he? Why did he attack me?"

She took my hand in hers and lowered her eyes. "He is my mate."

For a moment, the world seemed to dissolve into fire and ice. It could not be. She was mine. Mine!

"You did not wait for me!"

Tears stood in her lovely eyes. "I did. But it has been five years."

Two eons…so that was how it translated into human time. I had gambled – and lost. Between me and my happiness, stood another male. A human male.

She took my hand and placed it on her abdomen, where a small bulge rose under her dress. "I am carrying his child."

"Child?"

"A young one. Like me…or like him."

I looked from her to her mate. He glowered silently, only a few feet away.

"Leave him," I said. "Don't you know that I have become flesh for you?"

She shook her head sadly. "I cannot. I am his now. You came too late."

Weakness overcame me. I still had not eaten since my transformation. I began to tremble. The male used that moment to assert his dominance.

"Get out of my house you piece of filth. I don't want you near my wife again, do you hear?"

Weak though I was, I still had my fire, and I raised all my fury at once. She cried out when I pushed her from me, for I had singed her skin again. Yet it was him, I hated with all my might, him I dove for, and I wrapped my arms around his waist and held fast. I raged and bit and reveled in his screams, as I burned his flesh and tore at his throat.

He died quickly, and I feasted, until my strength returned. When I rose from the carnage, I saw her, huddled in a corner, eyes wide with silent fright.

Calmer now, I sat on the floor and called to her. "Come, kiss me. Let me share my warmth with you. Let my soul shine its light for you."

Her screams brought the villagers with pitchforks and clubs. Sating myself on the human had made me drowsy, and I did not grasp the danger until too late. Together, they subdued me and dragged me to their jail, where I now sit and await my doom.

In the days following my capture, I asked time and again to see her. When at last she came, she was dressed in long, black robes, and her eyes were red from crying.

"What do you want from me? You have slaughtered my mate. I hate you!"

"You do not hate me. You wish to be with me. We are joined, remember?"

"You are a monster. I would never lay with a monster."

"Yet you have lain with me. I have tasted you, and you have felt my passion."

She shuddered. Her eyes filled with loathing, as she remembered. How could she despise me? We were one.

"I never want to see you again. You will die, and I will be glad for it."

"But…you wanted it too…you kissed me first…out there on the forest path."

I noticed a small scar on her lower lip, where I once bit her. She saw me staring and covered her mouth with her hand. Without another word, she turned, walked from the jail, and never looked back.

I fell to my knees on the stone floor and spilled my light until my soul lay dim and weak inside me.

I did not regain my strength of fire. I poured out too much of it, and inside me only shadows remain. There is no need for me to suffer among humans, now that she is gone, but I cannot return home. My mind is clouded, and I cannot for the light of me remember how to vaporize. The art of transformation, a sprite's greatest boon, is lost to me. Demented, like a human, I sit in my cell and await death. And among the stones of this prison my love slowly drains away and yields to darkness.

Favorite Meal

"You fixed my favorite meal," said the ogre and, for once, looked pleased. With a mighty swing, he tossed his knapsack on the ground and plopped down on the tree stump to eat. He ate noisily, with much lip smacking and ran his tongue along his upper teeth in a way that made me want to retch.

Eating is what ogres seem to do best, although it is torture for civilized folk to watch them, even when we don't know what's in the stew. And I had been forced to watch him eat for weeks now, ever since my capture.

He spat out a Giant Mudgrub and it landed on my left foot, making me jump to shake it off before I'd feel its teeth rake across my flesh. Mudgrubs are poison to humans, even after they are cooked, and it had taken courage to collect the slimy things this morning in the bog.

"Not done enough!" he barked. I sighed. There was always something.

His name was 'Uggh' or something like that, rather difficult to pronounce. I had heard it a few times, but he made me address him with 'Master'. In my hatred of him, that seemed even harder to do.

I had cooked a big pot of stew, in hopes that he would eat for a long time. Perhaps he would go right to sleep and wouldn't make me clean out his toe nails after the meal.

"What's in the knapsack, Master?" I asked, not out of curiosity, but wary from experience. The sack was moving, and usually, he brought something dangerous.

He wiped his muzzle with the back of his hand and shook the droplets in my direction. I didn't dare duck.

"Open it up and see!"

I approached the knapsack cautiously, and he watched me with sadistic glee. Ever so slowly, I untied the string and eased open the mouth of the sack. Tempted by freedom, a furry head appeared, working its way out of the sack. I shrank back, but then...

"Fuzzy!" I cried, astounded and delighted, when my big orange tom cat squirmed out of the bag and scurried into my waiting arms. How did the ogre find him?

Fuzzy dissolved into a mass of purr, and I nuzzled him joyfully. I smiled up at the ogre through tears of gratitude, silently asking forgiveness for hating him so. There was some kindness in him after all.

"Lunch tomorrow," he said, and my heart turned to ice. I hugged Fuzzy against my chest and vowed secretly that it would never happen. This was the end of the line.

Gently, I put Fuzzy back into the knapsack and closed it. Determination and courage surged within me. When I stood to face the ogre, I had my emotions under control.

"Ready for seconds, Master?" I asked, deferentially, and he handed me his bowl without a word. I kept my back turned as I ladled the stew, hoping he wouldn't watch too closely. Quick as lightning, I slipped my hand into my pocket and retrieved the only thing I knew that could kill an ogre: talcum powder. I shook the whole bag into the bowl and stirred carefully. I had made the stew spicy enough to cover any scent or flavor the powder might impart.

He ate the whole bowl before he noticed. By then, the poison had seeped into his blood stream and was beginning to squeeze his evil heart. "Uggh," he gasped, clutching his chest, and I smiled at the irony of his name.

"Call to the giant Uggh in the eternal fire pit for all I care," I snapped, suddenly brave, while I watched all five hundred pounds of ogre sag to the ground. "I should have done this long ago."

Without looking back, I plucked Fuzzy out of the bag and headed down the road toward civilization. Fuzzy sat on my shoulder and hissed and spat viciously at the dying ogre.

The Trouble With Fairy Godmothers

Last Friday, I was finally fed up with my fairy godmother.

I'm not sure by what unlucky stroke of the pen I ended up with an embittered, sarcastic, and thoroughly unreasonable fairy godmother. Her name was unpronounceable and that exasperated her as much as it did me. I tried calling her Jean, but that didn't go over well, so we compromised and settled on Ana-sylph, still a tongue-twister, but at least capable of twisting my *human* tongue.

The trouble with fairy godmothers is that you can't pick the one you want. So when you end up with a nymph with a bad temper, she is apt to forget, what she was placed on this earth to do in the first place, namely, to grant wishes. Mine had been messing up my life since fifth grade.

I learned early not to trust Ana-sylph, but the real eye opener came the winter I turned ten, and my best friend Tom, his sister Lilly and I discovered that Duncan's Pond had frozen over. We walked to school and back in those days, and as chance would have it, our usual route was closed off due to construction. The alternate path was longer, steeper, but much more interesting. Duncan's Pond spooked us enough in summer, hidden away behind the wall of Duncan's Lair but in winter it was ultimately more frightening, because the dark, abandoned mansion beside it became so much more forbidding against the strange, gloomy shade under ancient, gnarled, exotic trees. And Duncan's Lair was straight up the hill ahead of us.

It was a test of courage to pass through the broken gates into the shadows, and we goaded each other to do it, any chance we could. I adored Tom, and I never let him outdo me, and neither did Lilly, who was just a year younger than the two of us, so when Tom veered off and began stomping through fresh powder toward the old gate, I knew we'd be in for an adventure.

We sneaked past the deserted manor, breath held in our throats, fearful, someone might be inside and see us trespass. Even though there were no cars in the courtyard and no tracks leading up to the door, one never knew with old buildings, whence the inhabitants might be arriving.

It was ghostly quiet inside the walls, and snow lay deep, but underneath the dry, powdery layer, it had packed down, and it crunched and squeaked under our steps. The moss, which scrambled up the tree trunks, had frozen, gracing itself with tiny, multi-rayed stars of blue-and-white frost. The path ran mostly uphill and we shuffled steadily upward toward the ridge, which surrounded Duncan's Pond. Tom reached the top first and stopped, enthralled with the view.

"It's frozen!" he called out, voice full of wonder, causing Lilly and me to scurry after him. Milk-white ice beckoned to us youngsters with our sense of adventure and our deplorable lack of good judgment.

"How thick is it?" I asked. "Do you think it will hold us?"

Tom turned and grinned, making my heart skip. "Let's go find out!"

I had wished for this, wished for this day with all my heart, for the ice and the adventure and to be with Tom and Lilly. I beamed.

"I'll race you there," I yelled and took off, snow scattering off my shoes, and white clouds of breath flying from my lips. I knew he would chase me; he always did. And he always caught me, being faster and all. I knew he would grab for me and knock me down in the snow and roll around with me, until we were both breathless and hot and thoroughly self-conscious, and then he would let me go and flop over on his back, laughing. I lived for those moments.

He didn't let me down. He caught me before I was even half-way to the ice. I landed with my face in wintry white, spitting and coughing, and he on top of me. I managed to fight my way out from under him and squirm out of his grip. I got my legs under me and pounced, gaining the upper hand. He grabbed me, even at that age already more muscular than I, but he didn't push me away. Our faces only inches apart, we giggled and panted, our innocent little ritual playing itself out in one of its charming variations, while Lilly stood, patiently waiting, eyes rolled skyward. *Here they go again…* Just as I had planned it.

What I didn't count on was Ana-sylph and that was a mistake. For in that moment, when we were still catching our breath, cheeks burning, aglow with contentment, she looked through my eyes and irrevocably and desperately fell in love with Tom.

It was bad enough that other girls at school begrudged us our friendship, but Ana-sylph's infatuation with my best friend was unethical, traitorous and downright creepy. It also turned out to be dangerous, at least for me.

The ice was thick. We tested it in several places, and when we were sure of its solidity, we ventured out on it, carefully at first, then more and more boldly. It was pure, unrivaled bliss. It was ignore-the-cold-and-the-falling-darkness ecstasy. It was forget-to-go-home-and-do-homework paradise.

"I wish I had my skates with me," I said, although my no-track soles worked quite well.

"Oh, I'll bet," Tom retorted. "So you can out-skate us all!"

"Speak for yourself!" Lilly said. "I can keep up with her."

"She can, Tom," I agreed, smiling. "Girls rule!"

Taking his cue, he set out to chase me again, this time on the ice. I squealed and took off toward the middle, where the ice was at its thickest. And that's when it happened.

I could hear Ana-sylph's nymphen laughter, the moment the ice gave under my feet and knew beyond a doubt that this was all her doing. I slid to a stop, when I felt the ground move, but it was too late. I know I screamed, and then the ice cracked, and I fell through. The freezing water instantly immobilized me. There was a moment of surprise and then only terror, when I felt suddenly heavy and realized that I could not stay afloat. I managed to get one good, deep breath, before I went down, the bitter cold stinging my face, after it already numbed my hands and feet.

"Help!" I tried to shout, but I was already under water, so nothing coherent came out. Somewhere under the gurgling of my escaping breath, I heard far-away voices, yelling, but I couldn't make out any words. I could see the opening in the ice above me. I was moving farther and farther away from it, down and over, following some invisible current. I was in dire need of air, and I knew I would drown, if I couldn't get to the surface, so I willed myself to move, against the petrified state of my body. It was no use. As much as I struggled, I no longer had the strength to reach the top. My lungs were about to burst and sharp pains shot through my ears into my head, as my ear drums froze. Understanding my predicament, I grew tranquil, knowing it was over, knowing I tried and failed. I stopped struggling. And then the miracle happened.

Strong arms reached down to grip me, haul me up and drag me to safety, across the breaking ice, onto the snow. Tom was over me, shouting, rubbing my face, arms and hands. Lilly was working vigorously on my legs, trying to get circulation started in them again.

"Come on, breathe!" Tom yelled, panic in his voice. I was already gasping in big gulps of air, but it took a moment for him to notice. As the blood returned to my extremities, pins and needles in my fingers and toes painfully reminded me that I was still alive. My lungs ached, and my head threatened to explode.

"Tom, it's ok, she's breathing," Lilly said. "Let's just get her warm." They crowded against me, from both sides, trying to thaw me out, to no avail. My clothes were soaked and were beginning to solidify in the crisp winter air.

I had to get up and moving. Lilly realized it too. "Uncle Chipper's house is closest," she said. "Come on, help me get her there."

They mostly dragged me through the snow to Chipper's old homestead. I sloshed and splattered with every step, my teeth chattered, and I shook so bad, I could hardly stay on my feet. It seemed a lifetime before we reached the front door.

Tom knocked and entered, holding the door open. "Go on inside," he said. "He won't mind."

Although Chipper was a strange character, we kids loved him. He was full of stories, and he knew more about the fairy world than anyone. He liked to tie one on, once in a while - his only weakness - so there was always whiskey in the house. And he was generous with it, another thing we kids appreciated.

"Make her a hot toddy," he told Tom now, while he tossed more wood into the fireplace. "And you, Lilly, get her in the shower. I'll take care of her clothes."

In the bathroom, Lilly helped me peel out of the cold, wet, and partially frozen garments and tossed them through the door at her uncle. She turned the shower on and checked to make sure it was not too hot.

"Stay in as long as you like. When you get through, you can wear Uncle Chipper's bath robe."

I nodded gratefully. It was the ugliest robe I had ever laid eyes on, but at this moment, I wouldn't have traded it for silk or satin. Gradually, I warmed up and my teeth stopped clattering. I dried off, wrapped up in the hideous robe and rejoined the others who had gathered around the fireplace. As I stepped into the room, I saw Ana-sylph, standing behind Tom's chair, worshipful eyes captivated by his smile. It was sickening. She spotted me and scowled. I stuck my tongue out at her and caught Chipper's knowing glance.

"Having some trouble with a nymph?" he asked.

I sighed. "Don't you know it! I think she tried to drown me."

Chipper grew serious. "That's actually quite possible. Perhaps she has an eye for our fellow Tom here and you're in her way."

"Eww!" Tom was not flattered. Who wants to be the love object of someone else's fairy godmother? That was the ultimate in cross-species obsession. Besides, Tom was only ten years old.

Lilly laughed out loud. "If she knew how disgusting you can be…"

"Shut up," Tom snapped. "You talk like a little sister."

We stayed at Chipper's house long enough for him to wash and dry my clothes. I sipped my hot toddy, wrapped in the old cotton robe and felt life return to my insides. So, my fairy godmother wanted me dead. What a concept!

"You'll have to outsmart her," Chipper advised. "It's best to be one step ahead of her at all times."

"How do I do that?"

"Well, for starters, you have to know what she likes and wants. And what she doesn't like. And you'll have to learn to anticipate her moves to fend off bad luck."

"Can't I just get rid of her?"

Chipper shook his head. "They're bonded to us for a lifetime. It's a trap for both sides. If you're lucky, you'll end up with riches and good fortune, but for most of us, they're more trouble than they're worth."

"So she's stuck with me too?" I was beginning to get the hang of this.

"Yep. That she is. And that's probably not going to make her happy."

At least I had some satisfaction, knowing that Tom was unattainable for Ana-sylph. She couldn't do anything for him, get near him, or grant him any wishes. What she could do and what she did consequently from that day on, was thoroughly screw up my life.

My problems were far from over that day. By the time I got home, it was dark, and my parents were frantic. I had planned to come up with a good lie to stay out of trouble, but Ana-sylph bumped me from behind, causing the truth to slip out, which earned me a solid whipping. I couldn't even keep the hot toddy a secret, since Momma smelled it, so I went to bed hungry, catching the aroma of the roasted lamb from my bedroom, where it made my mouth water. Cursed nymph!

Over the next ten years, unfortunate events kept happening to me. Sometimes, I was able to head them off, but not always. It was worst, when Tom was around. Luckily, Ana-Sylph wasn't too bright, or perhaps she was just distracted by her obsession with Tom, but I could easily confuse her with my wishes. If I wanted an A in history, I asked for an F, and if I wanted to go to a party, I'd ask for house arrest. Without fail, she would grant me the opposite, laughing spitefully, and I'd pretend to be angry. Sometimes, it backfired though, especially where Tom was concerned, and I embarrassed myself royally more than once.

In the summer of my eighteenth year, Lilly and I enrolled in the same college and became roommates. Tom, who had joined the Royal Guard, spent many an evening with us, talking, laughing, or on some crazy adventure. It was just like old times.

By and by, Ana-sylph's interference became a serious nuisance. When Tom and I began dating, the nymph turned exceedingly spiteful and mean. I once had to wear a wig for a whole year, because she switched my shampoo bottle with Lilly's hair remover. Then the roof leaked and thoroughly soaked only my side of the room. My ferret mysteriously caught the Avian Flu and my tax return was audited, year after year. And on and on it went.

When Tom asked me to marry him, things got out of hand. In a fit of jealousy, Ana-sylph cut my brakes and made me wreck my car. It was a miracle I walked away unhurt. It wasn't Ana-sylph's miracle though, because not even a week later, she tripped me and pushed me down the stairs. Lilly found me and called the paramedics.

This time, I wasn't so lucky. I fractured a hip and would have to stay in bed for four weeks, missing final exams. Tom and I had planned a trip to the coast this summer, and I had looked forward to sandcastles and long walks on the beach. Instead, I lay immobilized in a body cast, while summer happened without me. Tom stayed by my bedside. He was tender towards me, and I loved him more than ever. He and Lilly did what they could to make my life easier, but in the background, Ana-Sylph danced and frolicked.

I put a call in to Chipper to ask his advice. "She's going to kill me, Chip. I don't know what to do."

"Tell Tom, you can't marry him," he urged, deathly serious.

"What? I love Tom. And I *am* going to marry him. Tell me something else!"

"She's not going to let up. You can't outfox her. She'll get you sooner or later. You have to break it off with Tom."

"That's insane!" I hung up on him. I would handle my love-struck nymph my way.

But, last Friday, it all came to an end. That was the day, my pain medicine disappeared, and I was in agony. I knew the nymph had disposed of it, because she was laughing at me, taunting me and dancing around Tom, who searched the room.

"I'm sorry, honey," he said. "I'll find you some, even if I have to talk to every drug dealer in town."

He had brought me a steak dinner from the fancy diner off-campus, but I was in too much pain to eat. He bent over the bed to kiss me, all gentleness, love shining from his beautiful, deep brown eyes. In the corner of the room, I saw Ana-sylph glower. She moved and came towards us, fuming and determined. She would try to hurt me, again and again.

Suddenly, I had enough. All the years of dealing with her crashed down on me in that one excruciating moment, still frozen in time. I was finally and irreversibly fed up with her. And I thought of the one thing, the only thing I could do to make it all go away.

"I love you, Tom," I said, and then I plunged the steak knife between his ribs, through the lung, straight into his heart. I didn't miss. Anatomy was my favorite subject.

He collapsed in my arms, a look of shock and pain in his eyes, as his heart hemorrhaged into his lungs. He died quickly, suffocating on his own blood. I wept quietly with regret and rage and loneliness, but it was not quiet in the room. I can still hear the strangled sound of Tom trying to catch his last breath and, overshadowing it all, the keening, angry, desperate screams of the wretched nymph.

Lesser Glory

Yesterday:

"*The sun doesn't want to rise today. I loathe giving up one of my precious few days of adulthood to this gloom and pelting rain. When dragonflies hatch, the skies should be smiling. I try to smooth my wings, crinkled from damp and chill, my precious new wings, token of my sexual maturity. Will I ever fly?*

If only my distant ancestor had not been so full of greed and vanity! If only, in narcissistic self-glorification, he had not provoked and enraged the vengeful gods! I would still be breathing fire..."

She huddles miserably under a hyacinth leaf and watches her life drizzle away under charcoal skies. Like all dragonflies, she is born with knowledge of her wretched history. The legend is passed down from generation to generation in abject regret. She hides from her destiny and weeps for her species who once reigned over the earth, and whose awe-inspiring powers have faded into oblivion...

Today:

"*The sun has seen fit to come out and greet me. She feels as wonderful as I imagined. I dry my wings in her radiance and want to melt with adoration. My heart sings – no, it is my wings that sing! Instinctively, I move them, and they buzz and vibrate with stored energy. How splendid they look in daylight! The dragons of our ancient past could not boast of such colors.*"

She flies to the water and perches atop a blade of reed grass. Wings aspread, she hovers silently, weightlessly. She admires her reflection in the still water. Aquiver with anticipation, she scans the horizon. Her second day of adulthood promises boundless joy.

"Why did I cry last night? Did any dragon ever find such primal pleasure? Perhaps when we lost our might, we found a greater treasure still. To sail lightly on the wind, to live in perfect splendor, how could I wish for more?"

In the distance, she spots something, a sparkle at water's edge, flicking this way and that. Wings even more magnificent than her own catch her eye and she takes flight eagerly to meet the creature which basks in the sun's rays. Together, they dance in playful self-indulgence and mate, as nature intended. And finally, she forgets about dragons, fire, and faded glory.

Unhappily Ever After

Princess Miriam sat in her chamber by the window, contemplating murder.

She had been sitting there for half an hour, alone with her sinister thoughts, when a movement caught her attention in the meadow below. The tall, handsome man who dashed up the hillside made her heart skip. He didn't look up, since he fancied her still asleep, but if he had, he would have seen her cling to the window, gazing down at him with longing. Always the gentleman, he was dressed in a dark suit and carried flowers, lilacs, knowing they were her favorites.

She watched him make a wide circle to avoid the temptation of the lily pond. She had kissed him out of a frog just a little over three years ago, and he still had trouble abandoning his amphibian ways. He tried to hide his beastly quirks, so as not to remind her of his past, but he wasn't very cunning, and his true nature had a tendency to slip through.

After too many years in the lily pond, he disliked sleeping in a soft, dry feather bed. Miriam heard him toss and turn at night. Sometimes, restlessness drove him out of bed and into the bath where he lingered for hours.

He loved the rain. He stared out the window wistfully during a downpour. The summer drought made him moody and caused his skin to itch and peel.

He was jumpy and easily caught off-guard, but not very watchful. She was surprised, he had survived his frog years. There were predators aplenty in the castle park, and many of them preyed on the inhabitants of the lily pond.

The hinges screeched when the door opened downstairs, and she scurried back into bed. He should find her there, sleeping. She heard a rustle in the room and smelled the heady perfume of the lilacs which he laid beside her on the covers. She opened her eyes.

"Good morning, Princess." He always called her that, and she was still not used to it. She couldn't help but smile.

Her joy was genuine. "Oh, they are beautiful! Thank you, Donovan. You are so thoughtful."

Being in his presence always triggered her insecurity. She was hopelessly smitten with him and could get lost in his eyes in a flash. Just now, when he bent over her for his morning kiss, she felt breathless like a school girl. She hoped he would take her in his arms and make love to her, but his manners showed a touch of formality.

"I trust you had pleasant dreams?" he inquired.

"Thank you," she said, "How kind of you to ask." If only he knew!

Prince Donovan smiled. "The flower show will open in less than two hours. I'll send for the maid to help you get ready."

Of course! As crown princess, she was obligated to judge the show. She had almost forgotten it was today. She didn't mind, really. The bustle of getting ready would disguise her plot.

On the surface, there was no reason for her unholy musings. Prince Donovan showered her with gifts and did his best to fulfill her every wish. She, who had once been wretchedly poor, now dressed in silk and satin and dined royally every day and every day in his presence.

Her duties in the kingdom were light and pleasant, now that peace reigned eternally. She was popular, and when she appeared on Sundays on Donovan's arm, looking all regal and polished, the crowds cheered and threw flowers at her feet. The gallant prince was ever at her service, his chivalry soothing after years of maltreatment at the hands of her wicked stepfather, but despite his constant attention, Miriam sensed, something was missing.

The prince opened the door for the chambermaid now, who entered and curtsied prettily before the royal couple.

"Please help my wife get ready," he said. "She hasn't much time."

The chambermaid respectfully ushered Miriam toward the bathroom, where a giant, gilded tub awaited her, gardenias floating on the water.

"Highness, please be careful not to slip," she clucked.

Miriam smiled a grateful smile. She sank into the hot, fragrant bath and closed her eyes, giving herself over to the chambermaid's ministrations. What was her name? Cara? Carmen? Carina!

"Carina, do you think the prince is handsome?"

It was not something one would ask a chambermaid, normally, but Miriam, born a commoner, didn't always follow the rules.

"Your Highness," stuttered the maid, "I'm not entitled to say."

"Of course not…forget I asked." Coming from humble beginnings herself, Miriam wouldn't have been entitled either, had it not been for the kiss. A prince always keeps his promise, even if he is a frog when he makes it.

Carina helped her into the beautiful off-white silk dress and matching shoes. Miriam liked understated elegance and did not care for flamboyancy, which seemed to please the prince. He complimented her often and sincerely, making her eyes shine.

"I think he is dreadfully handsome," Miriam exclaimed. "I must be the luckiest woman in the world."

"Your Highness, I'm sure Prince Donovan considers himself even luckier."

Was there a touch of insincerity in the chambermaid's voice? Was her appraisal of the prince's physical attributes just a slight too casual? Her flattery a tad overdone?

Miriam stopped herself short, ashamed of her suspicions, but over the past months, a growing anxiety had been building within her, birthed by a sudden insight into the amphibian soul of her beloved husband.

Prince Donovan did not love her. She knew it as surely as she knew her own enamored heart. And she feared he had romantic feelings for someone else.

Sure, the prince gushed with gratitude and attention, and he never gave her a harsh word. He was a gentle, tender lover, those rare times when he approached her, and he brought her fresh flowers almost daily.

But a woman knows. And so her thoughts grew lethal.

She had followed him a few times, when he was unaware. Heart thumping painfully, high in her throat and barely breathing, she sneaked, hiding in the shadows, unworthy of a princess. But that tight, worm-wiggling feeling in her belly was not rewarded, as he gave her the slip each time. Finally, she consulted a sorceress, hoping for relief.

"Give me something to still my imagination. I have no cause to distrust the prince."

The sorceress waggled her head back and forth. "But, perhaps you do."

Lightning seemed to strike Miriam's heart, and she felt faint. "What are you saying, witch?"

And then they hatched out a plan.

"Two potions, Highness, one renders you invisible, the other reveals the truth. Use them wisely. The first you drink, the second you keep. You'll know what to do when the time comes."

Carina combed Miriam's long, wild, stubborn tresses and piled them loosely up on her head, pinning them as well as she could to force them into submission. Miriam watched the maid in the mirror, willed herself to imagine her in Donovan's arms, found it possible.

"Enough," she said, raising her hand so abruptly, the maid dropped the comb. "Leave me."

Eyes closed and breath held against the stench of it, she swallowed the potion. It burned as it went down, and she had to suppress a retching. Minutes later, her door opened and closed again, yet the maid, who waited outside her room, saw no one pass through.

Invisible, Miriam crept down the broad marble stairs, through the hall and to her husband's study. He was not there. Systematically, she searched all the rooms.

She had about two hours before the potion would wear off.

In the stables, she found him at last, whispering soft words into a lover's ear. She wanted to scream, to accuse, to cry, but found herself in a tongue-tangling fury. Without a thought, she opened the second potion and threw it at the pair, its contents spilling over the prince and his consort. As she did, her own spell vanished, and she stood, visible to the angry eye.

What the flash of light revealed, finally freed her tongue. The young, wayward husband of the sorceress, face flushed from passionate tryst, only partially clothed, cried his anguish, and she joined him in wailing, when she bent to retrieve what was left of Prince Donovan: A large, green, slippery frog, croaking, as she held him, struggling to get free, all his frog senses drawing him toward the nearby lily pond.

She covered his cold, wet body with kisses, but the magic didn't work anymore. How long would it take? Twenty years? A Hundred?

"What have you done?" cried the prince's lover. "He was the world to me!"

"I didn't know, I swear it!"

He took the frog from her, gently, lovingly and carried him to the pond to release him. Without looking back, he followed him into the water, step by despairing step, until the pond opened up and swallowed him, leaving behind only ripples.

Not courageous enough to follow, Princess Miriam knelt in the grass by the edge and sobbed, while, miles away, the sorceress savored her bittersweet vengeance.

The guards searched for the prince for a Hundred and Eighty days, before they proclaimed him dead. Neither he nor his lover was ever seen again.

From her window, Miriam watches the lily pond every day now, searching for a small, green creature. Under the worried eyes of the chambermaid she has wasted away to a shadow of her former self. She would welcome death now, yet every morning she wakes, alive for yet another day, and she weeps, living unhappily ever after in a room, filled with lilacs.

Norelle

"Magic beans?" Chris laughed, until his sides ached. "How old are you anyway?

She shrugged. It was a lovely gesture, somewhat forlorn and child-like. "I'm not sure. We stop counting after the first two hundred years."

She was pulling his leg. She must be.

"What's your name?" he asked, not sure why he cared.

"You can call me Norelle."

"Norelle? Is that your real name?"

She shook her head. "You can't pronounce my real name. It's…foreign."

Perhaps she was French. He had to admit, that intrigued him. "Try me."

"Tchktkpvuelsyty," she said and it sounded as though she coughed up a hairball.

"Norelle it is!" He regarded her with suspicion. "So what's the deal with these beans?"

She sighed. This one was particularly dense. "You plant them - they grow."

Irritated, he said "That's not magic!"

Humans! She though. *Ever the skeptics.* She tossed the beans out, in a wide arch across the ground. A ray of sparks sprang up from where they touched earth, spraying as high as three feet and as far as six or seven. Some of them hit Chris, and he jumped, his flesh singed. Norelle stood in the middle of the shower, still looking lovely.

Almost instantly, the beans began to sprout, growing long, finger-like shoots of an undefined color. Lightning-fast, they snaked around Chris, still growing, until they had him wrapped up in vines. When they began to squeeze, he screamed. And he screamed until they squeezed the air right out of him, and he heard his ribs crack. Within minutes, there was nothing left but a large pile of bean plants, spread out over the ground.

"Magic," said Norelle and her voice had an I-told-you-so quality.

She waited until the beans were ripe and picked them, a bucket full. Smiling with the innocence of a young child, she skipped away, possibly toward her next victim.

The Veils

Journal entry:
According to the old timers, we never should have killed off the dragons.

Never mind that our cattle now graze openly in the meadow, never mind that we dare build houses from wood and straw again, and never mind that the children are unafraid to play outdoors during the daytime. Our village seniors never stop grumbling.

"There is a place in nature for everything," they say. "Even for a dragon."

Sure. Dragons don't eat old dried-up, leather-skinned townsmen. They are after us young, tasty ones with the tender flesh and the sweet smell of copulation. What do the elders know of the fleeting nature of a lover's tryst, overshadowed not only by the thought of being caught by our parents, but the realistic fear of being singed and devoured in the middle of our passionate embrace? Surely they have long since forgotten the smoldering desire for another's touch and never knew the screaming agony of a second and third degree burn, like the one branded across my back. I can still smell the stench of my own charred skin.

I saved myself, but my lover was not so lucky. The dragon's breath merely touched me, but she was engulfed in flames.

The old timers are getting senile. We should not listen to them rant.

Yesterday, I picked up my journal and read again my words from two years past, and it occurred to me, how often we speak or make life-altering decisions without enough insight. Oh how I wish I could eat my words now!

There is a change in weather coming. The scars on my back itch mercilessly, reminding me once again of my personal agony. Today I am experiencing one of my saner moments, so I am able to write lucidly, without too many hallucinations.

It is difficult, these days, to distinguish truth from imagination. The Veils have seen to that. The air is filled with ethereal white apparitions. Every day there seem to be more of them, their ubiquitous presence haunting our every move. If only they were quiet! I could live with their ghostly appearances, their cold, wet, slippery touch, with which they assault us anywhere, anytime, even in our most private moments, if only they could not speak.

No one really knows how they enter our minds, how their presence translates into words and phrases, how they trigger us into action. We have all but eliminated social structure, living fearfully in seclusion, afraid of what our neighbors might do to us, while under the influence.

I haven't touched my wife intimately in months, not since I caught myself, unconsciously fitting my hands around her slender neck, wanting to squeeze. Most of us live bizarre, lonely lives with memory lapses and borderline personality disorders. And all of us live in fear of losing our minds.

The Veils began emerging soon after the dragons disappeared. There weren't but a few of them then, strange, eerie phenomena, and nobody saw the connection yet. Jack Dillinger of the morning news was the first to report seeing them, and he was promptly placed on medication and in a straight jacket. For a while, folks kept quiet, fearing a similar fate, but then the voices began to worry them, and they came forward in great numbers.

Six months ago, the Veils invaded the city. First, we felt them, ghost-like in the night, brushing against us, then we heard their spine-chilling howls. Then, suddenly, they were everywhere. I placed a call to the health department.

"What are they? Where do they come from? And why are there so many of them?"

The clerk was congenial, but unable to answer my questions. "Perhaps you should call the State University, she suggested, "and talk to someone in the veterinary research department."

Yesterday, I did that, and what they told me, made my blood chill.

"Veils are organic life-forms," said the researcher, "but we are not sure how they metabolize energy. They have a parasitic effect only on the brains of mammals. When they touch us, they insert their DNA through the skin into our blood stream. It travels to the brain, where it re-wires neural circuits and creates hallucinations."

"That would explain the visions, but what about the other personality changes?"

"Veil DNA over-stimulates the primitive part of the brain, where emotions are born and brings about violent and anti-social behavior."

That made sense to me. Biology was at least tangible. I could wrap my wounded mind around it.

"Is there a cure?"

And that was the bad news. Once infected, the course of the disease is always fatal.

Prevention? No chance of that either: "Veil DNA mutates every few hours," the scientist said, "and we can't lock down a gene long enough to develop a vaccine."

Poison baits and sprays don't affect the Veils either. And indestructible, except by fire, these vaporous, wraith-like apparitions are adept at avoiding flames.

I had one last question. I needed to know why they were here and why in such numbers. Only one reason came to mind and I wanted to be wrong about this. The time sequence was unmistakable, the conclusion had to be drawn, like it or not. And so I asked, eyes tightly closed, trying to will away the truth.

The researcher showed no mercy. "It appears," he said, "that they only have one natural enemy, and that enemy has become extinct."

"Yes," I whispered, knowing the answer, understanding how I had become part of humanity's ruin. I, with my raving and my hatred, driven by my loss and the indelible scars on my back, I had become the instrument of my own destruction, paying an excruciating price each day, as I now live in fear and isolation. I had been vocal and leading in the crusade, and I had done my share of killing.

It appears, in the end, that the old timers were right. If only we had listened. If only we had believed. I know the truth now, painfully obvious. They were right to warn us. We never should have killed off all the dragons.

THE WAVE

Paul Rider stared at his pitiful puddle of a stock pond and gnawed his lower lip. Muddy hoof prints by the water were beginning to dry, and there would be drink for only a few more days for his hundred head of cattle. He'd be trucking water in soon. At current gas prices, it would put a big dent in his budget. He might even have to take half his herd to the auction.

But then, he had an idea. It was a crazy idea, but it just might work.

He had heard surfers use the phrase 'to catch a wave,' but Paul was not a surfer. He was a shrewd businessman and creative thinker. If a wave could be caught, it could also be captured. And if he fed it well, he should be able to grow it big enough to fill his pond.

But what did a wave need for nourishment? Sand? Coral? Fish? Wind maybe? Paul tapped frustrated fingers on his mouse pad when the Internet revealed nothing. Had no one tried this before?

He had a few days to figure out the particulars but he would have to act soon. He packed for an overnight journey and kissed Lori, his wife, tenderly.

"I'll be back in day or two."

She raised a suspicious brow. "Where are you going so early? The auction doesn't start until tomorrow."

"I have to check on some cattle down in Houston," he lied. He didn't trust her with the truth. She'd think he was nuts. "You can come with me if you want."

But Lori hated travel and shook her head as expected. "I'd rather hang out with the cows."

Paul drove the big Ford dually, loaded with shovels, boards, ropes and chains, and pulled a trailer with a Thousand gallon tank. In three hours, he reached Galveston and headed straight for the harbor, to the pub where the locals drank on Friday afternoons. He had to spring for a few rounds before the fishermen lost their wariness.

"What do you feed a wave?" he asked when a couple of burly, bearded seamen invited him to their table.

"Your soul," said one. "Old Dave Murphy caught a wave once. It can be done, but I don't recommend it. The wave ate his soul."

But Paul only heard the possibility, not the warning. "How did he do it?"

And after a couple more rounds, they told him in detail about the business of trapping waves. And they told him how to make a wave give up its salt by dowsing it with sugar.

"You're in luck. It's New Moon tomorrow."

"New Moon?" Paul didn't make the connection.

"It causes a Spring Tide."

A Spring Tide with lower lows and higher highs…

The fisherman nodded. "It will help with the catching…but it also brings more danger."

Paul grinned. "I like a challenge."

The fishermen puffed on their pipes and hid behind smoke rings.

The next day, Paul found a spot on the beach far enough from housing to remain undisturbed, measured out the projected tidal current and began to dig. The waters were slack and turning. He had time.

The sea wind blew cool and gentle air across the sandy expanse. Still, all the digging made him sweat, and he soon worked in just boots and boxers. He had labored all his life, and muscles rippled lean and hard under his tanned skin. Fine blond hairs covered arms, legs, and chest and redirected sweat rivulets into streams and rivers along his body. He glistened, and in the slack time the ocean watched – and admired.

When he was satisfied with digging, Paul backed the trailer into the trough, letting the edge of the water tank sit just below the rim of sand. He smoothed the beach on sea side and realigned the dually. He put up his shovel and rested.

Paul loved the sea. As a child, he had lived near her, before his father bought the ranch. He knew how to fish and could skip a seashell far onto quiet water. He slipped out of his boots and waded into the rising tide. Surf was up, and white crests danced over dark ripples all the way to the horizon. His bare feet crunched over tiny shells, piled on the sand bank like treasures. He picked up a small oyster shell, weighed it, but didn't skip it. The sea was too rough.

He could sense the tide roll in, like something tugging at his insides. The odor of fish and salt hung in the air and tickled his senses. A tanker hovered right below the skyline, a black pause amidst restless brilliance. Another approached from the left, dragging thick, gray smoke. Paul fidgeted. There was a wave out there with his name on it; he just knew it.

A chill in the afternoon air made him dress in a hurry. He checked his watch; it was getting close. His stomach growled, he hadn't eaten since morning, but there was no time. Once more he checked his trap, made sure the truck sat on solid ground and that the trailer hitch held fast. He paced. He scanned the horizon. He made sure he wasn't being watched. He paced.

Inquisitive waves began to creep upward, reaching for familiar ground and edged ever so slowly toward Paul's trap.

"Come on," he whispered, hunter's instinct afire, "You know you want it."

But the waves courted Paul as well, and he noticed that even if he moved back a step or two, there they were, lapping at his feet again. How convenient!

He wanted a young wave, but a full one, reasonably sized and of a good quality and strength, so it would survive the transport and not die on the highway. He teased the approaching water, dancing forward and backward and to the side, away from the pit, until he felt that the sea had built up enough force to fill the tank with just one wave. And then he ran to the truck and started the engine.

The ocean roared after him and washed over the pit, dousing the truck with salt spray. A wave, a single, beautiful white-crested daughter of the ocean tumbled from the beach into the hidden tank and sloshed against its heavy steel sides. Paul screamed in triumph and slammed the Ford in gear. With one giant roar of the powerful engine, he dragged the tank out of the pit and away from the water's edge. He stopped and dashed back to cover the tank with boards and secure it to the trailer. The wave inside splashed against the tank walls, seeking to escape. Her voice gurgled in the steel container.

The deceived ocean realized her loss and rose in anger. Harnessing the wind, she whipped up breakers tall enough to swallow a ship and threw herself across the sandy bank toward Paul and his wet captive. Paul leapt into the truck and raced away, flinging sand from his wide, deeply treaded tires. The Ford howled in protest until it reached the road and gripped paved surface. With an anxious look in the mirror, Paul scanned a rapidly darkening sky and broke every speed limit, as he rushed toward interstate and safety. Behind him, the sea churned and hated.

Halfway home, Paul stopped at a rest area and checked the tank. The wave sat wan and miserable in her iron prison. She had dropped her foam crest and undulated silently. Paul worried.

"Don't you crap out on me! We still have a long way to go."

The wave slapped metal, making it clank.

Energy, he thought. It feeds on energy. And he closed his eyes and focused.

He felt his strength drain, while the wave picked up movement and began to roll. When his knees buckled, he tore away, startled, and hung over the truck bed, panting. The wave stirred and sloshed in a cold rage. Paul backed away and crept into the truck. His head ached.

The radio warned of a sudden, severe storm. The sea had come to furious life, determined to get revenge. But Paul escaped northward, speeding on interstate, with his trailer swaying precariously.

Night had fallen when he reached the ranch. Lovely Lori stood in the doorway barefoot, long hair flowing in the breeze and pointed at the water trough. He wanted to rush up, sweep her into his arms and tell her the whole crazy story, but he still had work to do. So he honked and rolled down the window.

"I'll go water the calves. I'll be right in Honey!"

He raced to the stock pond, backed the trailer just to the rim of the muddy water and released the wave. She flushed out of the container with barely concealed ferocity and licked along the pond's edges, looking for sand. She smelled the brackish water but didn't taste salt. Her foam crests flew up like lather from a rabid dog's mouth. She crashed toward the bottom of the pond. And realized the betrayal!

Irate, she hurled herself against the banks. In the hoof prints, small eddies formed, as she churned about. She shouted her rage to the wind, and the wind picked up her fury and howled across the pasture, slamming Paul against the side of his truck. Feeding off the wind, the angry wave thrashed around and built momentum. She whipped up white froth and tossed it over the banks onto the trampled grass. The longer she raged, the more maddened she became, and the wind, her accomplice nourished her wrath. Paul tried to escape to the truck, but the wave threw herself between him and his shelter and chewed at his buckling legs.

"Help! Lori, help me!"

But the wind screamed louder, and the wave leapt up and filled his mouth with foam and salt just before ripping loose his feet and slamming him down into the rolling water, where he bit into mud and cow patties.

The wave washed over him, pinned down his arms and legs and filled his lungs with wet, stinking death. She knew she was dying but she would take down this human who captured her and smother him with her weight. She held on until he stopped struggling. Then she sank back and rested.

When Lori ran through the night with a flash light, calling his name, Paul was already dead. He lay face down in the mud at the edge of his pond. Dark water gently undulated with the quieting wind.

Lori pulled Paul to dry land and wept. She shook him, patted his face and covered him with kisses. Her voice rose high into the night with a wail so wretched, the wind held its breath and fell silent.

"Paul, Paul, please don't leave me! Come back to me!" But it was too late.

In the depth of the stock pond, the dying wave felt no remorse.

Loraleigh

At night
When fish sleep
Finally free
From her daily duties
Mermaid – Nursemaid
To the schools
Of the deep seas
Half girl only
And Lonely
She combs her long hair
On a rugged rock
And sings

At dusk, a green-gray sea spewed brackish spray over Loraleigh, who sat on a jagged rock, nude, but for her scaled fish tail and sang. Her hair, grown to waist length during her tenure, resisted her cold fingers, when she tried to part it and comb out the tangles. Irritated, she squeezed out the hated salt water, but the smell of fish still clung to her and made her gag and retch.

At night, the fish slept, suspended in darkened water and safe from predators, and she, the nursemaid, was free for a while. At night, she came to the surface to gulp in breaths of precious air, although her lungs ached and burned each time she filled them. At night, she raised her voice and poured her anguish into a song, which ghosted over waves until it crashed ineffectively into tall, rugged cliffs.

It was spring. She felt as restless as the sea. Memories of another life haunted her, images and feelings she could no longer put into words, but they were just as vivid as ever. She had walked on two legs before. She was sure of it. She remembered the sensation of solid ground under her feet; she remembered holding someone's hand, warm and tender, remembered lips pressed against her lips. Yes, she was human once.

A wave crested over her rock, and she flapped her tail angrily. Cold rivulets ran down between her breasts and pooled in her small, round navel. She stared at her belly, at the smooth transition from girl to fish. Once warm and vibrant, she had become a creature of the deep, and her transformation had left her sexless. What a price to pay for moments of careless vanity!

A ship's horn sounded in the distance, and her song rose to meet it. A tired seaman labored aboard, securing the lines and stopped when he heard her. An ache stirred in his soul and in his loins as well. He had been at sea a long time.

"Mermaids," he murmured, but then it was just the wind. He stepped into the warm safety of his cabin and closed the door. He didn't believe the legends.

Loraleigh slipped quietly into the rolling sea. Mermaid - by a slip of the tongue they called her that. Lucidly, she recalled the day when she fell for a handsome stranger who promised to make her beautiful, so all men would admire her. She meant to model on stage, not nursemaid Cichlids and Krill. Should she have guessed where he would take her?

She shot through turbulent water. Her muscular tail undulated, propelling her snakelike toward the distant ship. She would not give up so easily. The seaman, who stared through his cabin window at the angry sea, gasped as he saw her floating in the water, naked and beautiful, beside his ship.

"Woman overboard!" he yelled and ran for the rail. For a moment, he stared. When he tossed her a life preserver, she moved away, seemingly treading water. And then she sang again, music without words, until the big, burly seaman wept.

"Take me with you! Save me from the fish and the King of the Deep!" she tried to shout, but only a single note floated up to torture his lonely heart. The sweetness of her song crushed his sanity, and he tore off his clothes. Without a single rational thought, he leapt over the rail and plunged into the raging ocean.

Loraleigh slipped cold, almost human arms around him and drew him into a kiss. His hands were everywhere, on her face, in her hair, on her breasts, until they reached her ample hips. He screamed when he felt her fish tail and flailed to get away when he realized what she was. For a moment, she relented in surprise, and he cursed and struck her hard across her lovely face.

She shrieked like a banshee and smacked him violently with her powerful tail. It only took one good swish to break his neck. Her left hand buried in his hair, and she pulled him down into the deep water and toward a cove where sharks lived. She watched gleefully, while they tore her gift to pieces, leaving the crystal waters of the cove soiled with blood.

Her hatred of everything fish and everything human did not sustain her for very long. Limp like a rag doll, she floated to the surface beside her secluded rock. And in the cold, stormy night she wept bitterly, for the dead seaman and for her lost humanity.

Dragon Keeper

It was in all the papers. Tanner had bought three of them, all daily rags from the area, each trying to outdo the other with gaudy headlines and graphic pictures. All other news was confined to the back, since the zoo took front page. After all, there hadn't been a dragon born in nearly thirty years.

"They are going to drive her mad!" he grumbled, as he studied the picture of the she-dragon, wings aspread, steam shooting from flared nostrils.

Tanner had begged and pleaded with the board to wait with the press release, but they insisted that the zoo needed publicity to get out of the red numbers. And the press had responded eagerly and with enthusiasm.

When Tanner was young, dragons had roamed freely in the distant hills. Smaller than in the old days and more docile, their numbers dwindled, a consequence of their changing diet and habitat. Pressed hard by the ever advancing human civilization, they had become predominantly vegetarian, only occasionally feasting on a lost sheep or a careless rabbit. With their reclusive ways, they were no threat to humans, so young Tanner was surprised when the Fish and Game Commission suddenly opened season.

Once an avid hunter, he was quick to learn the craft of killing dragons, and he soon amassed an impressive collection of crest-shaped scales on his trophy wall. In his twenties, he became a guide, making his living by leading hunting expeditions and teaching others how to pursue the more and more elusive exotic game.

"On the one hand, it is much like hunting a bear," he explained. "Make sure your caliber is big enough, and you hit your target right on, or you'll only make him furious. But on the other hand, it's much harder, because dragons are intelligent and can out-smart you."

City-folk, who hired him for the adventure, listened in rapt attention, but rarely managed to make a good, clean kill, crippling many a dragon and making it wary of any human presence. Deeper and deeper into the hills the fiery beasts retreated, leaving behind trails of ashes and destruction, as they vented their futile anger and their ever rising despair. Much like the whales, who once sang their anguish in a dying sea, they called their eerie shrieks across the hilltops, quaking the hearts of all who heard them.

When sightings became rarer than those of the timid mountain lions, environmental groups at last took an interest in the vanishing dragons' plight. They built zoos and habitats and hired Tanner to capture the alluring livestock. Accustomed to killing, he damaged quite a few specimens before learning to trap them alive, but eventually, he became the leading expert on dragon preservation.

As often happens, his extended personal involvement with the mystical creatures evoked a deep caring. Ashamed of his part in causing their demise, he locked away his scale collection and dedicated the second half of his life to fervent atonement. Eventually, he came to oversee several zoos, where he ensured the wellbeing of the captured dragons, while he studied their social structure and mating habits. He gave weekly talks on the radio and was frequently interviewed and quoted by the press.

While Tanner had the expertise, he didn't control the money, and despite his vocal protests, the zoo board allowed photographers and hundreds of visitors into the dragon keep, immediately after the hatching.

Out of seven eggs, only two hatched and one of the hatchlings was deformed from inbreeding. The zookeepers immediately removed and destroyed the crippled dragon, while its mother was away, feeding. The remaining, healthy one was displayed and paraded, drawing visitors from all directions and giving the zoo its much needed boost.

"Please be quiet and refrain from flash photography," Tanner called out, as he took yet another group to the keep. "The newly hatched dragon is a very sensitive and delicate creature. Too much noise creates stress and may cause failure to thrive."

"He looks healthy enough to me," one of the visitors said. "I always heard that it takes an act of God to kill a dragon."

"A fully grown dragon is difficult to kill," Tanner agreed, "but the little ones barely have any scales yet, and their nervous system is not fully developed."

"Really?" asked a woman. "How do they survive in the wild?"

"The youngsters stay with their mother until they fledge and can fend for themselves, and no predator is fool enough to get between a she-dragon and her chick."

Several children ran over to the enclosure and began to beat on the glass. The dragon chick bleated and scurried to hide under its mother's wing.

"Please keep your kids close to you," Tanner pleaded. "They have already frightened the chick. And move to the back, once you've had a look, so someone else can see. We'll be leaving soon. The mother won't tolerate our presence much longer."

But there were too many people in the keep and too many unruly children. There were at least ten of them now, beating on the glass in unison. The she-dragon rose, pushing her chick behind her and flapped her massive wings. Her crest flared as she arched her long, graceful neck, signaling a warning. With her back pressed against the artificial cliff, her only escape was forward. She let out an ear curdling shriek.

"Step back," Tanner yelled, sensing the danger. "Her belly heat is rising. She'll soon breathe fire."

Right about then, someone flashed a picture, eager to catch the beast in her fury. Tanner leapt forward and knocked the camera out of the man's hand. "No flash!" he yelled, but it was too late. The dragon, momentarily blinded, rocked her head from side to side, trying to identify the perpetrator. The flash represented fire to her and fire meant danger. To Tanner's demise, it was his face she saw, when her vision cleared and his fist, brandishing the now broken camera in the visitor's face.

Her first blast of heat shattered the supposedly fire-proof glass, felling humans under its blistering fallout. With her claws, she pushed out the remaining shards, her eyes trained on Tanner, as she stepped through. Those, who were able, ran screaming for the doors, but Tanner saw too late that he had become a target. Instinctively, he threw up his arms to shield his face.

"No!" he cried, fearing for himself, but also for his protégé and her endangered species, but he couldn't stop her. With one scorching, flaming, searing breath, she reduced to ashes the one and only human willing and able to protect her, thus sealing her own fate and that of her vanishing kind.

Zookeepers stormed the building. Under the assault of their machine guns, the dragon fell, mortally wounded. Drunk with killing, they shot the chick as well, having proof now, that it was too dangerous to let any of them live. They destroyed the remaining eggs, just to be safe. They didn't stop until the whole habitat lay in ruins, while from the shelter of the outside corridor a rogue newsman excitedly took pictures.

The Shoe Princess

When Nikki slipped off her bar stool and tossed a careless tip on the bar, instead of meticulously stuffing it in the bartender's tip jar, she had no idea that her life was about to make a complete turn-around.

She stopped by the Ladies' room on her way out and stepped up to the mirror to check her appearance. She wore only a minimum of makeup, and chestnut colored hair framed her face and brought out her beautiful, almond-shaped green eyes. The merest suggestion of crow's feet hinted at a life well lived, but didn't distract from her smooth complexion or her striking attractiveness. She smiled. Not bad for fifty-two.

She had to fumble for her keys and she wasn't sure where she had parked her classy white Lancia. Luckily, she had recently added electronic locks, and the touch of a button revealed the car's location. Amidst the modern vehicles on the lot, the Lancia exuded an understated elegance. Nikki ran a caressing hand over the hood. This was her second go-round with this particular car, and this time, she'd hold on to it. After having owned and driven nearly every luxury car a rich industrialist felt compelled to acquire, she had spent a small fortune to find the elegant and sporty Italian her father had bought her for her sixteenth birthday, and which she had so carelessly traded in, the day after he died.

Nikki swayed a little, but slipped into the driver's seat anyway. The engine sprang to life and purred. Nikki shifted into gear and pulled out of the lot, but before she fully accelerated, a woman jumped out into the street and waved her arms frantically. Nikki stomped the brake pedal and came to a screeching halt – not soon enough: she felt a sickening 'thud,' and the stranger dropped out of sight to the ground.

Nikki leapt from the car and hurried to the fallen woman's side. Frantically, she tried to remember her first aid skills. It had been years since she had taken a class. While she checked the woman for breathing and pulse, she steadily prayed to anything in the universe that might listen and might grant her just this one favor, perform this one miracle and take back the fact that she had just killed someone.

So far, no one had heard the impact. No one had stepped outside the bar or opened any windows to investigate the commotion. As much as Nikki wanted to call for help, she was also afraid. She didn't want to be associated with a dead body.

Flee! Get in the car now and escape and no one will ever know! But Nikki had a conscience and a compassionate heart. She couldn't leave the stranger on the cold, gray street. Without much thought, she opened the passenger door and began to drag the woman's body to the car. The stranger didn't weigh much. She must not have seen a decent meal in quite some time. Nikki, who spent hours at the gym every week, managed to heave her into the passenger seat without too much trouble. With the dead stranger buckled into the seat beside her, Nikki sped away toward the open highway.

Perhaps it was the alcohol or maybe her eccentric lifestyle had dulled her senses toward reality, but the full impact of what she had done didn't hit her until she snaked up the curvy mountain road thirty minutes later. She had carefully avoided looking at the body slumped beside her, but now she stole a look at the pale, blue-tinged woman and realized, she was sitting in the car with a corpse.

She screamed. She began to shake. She could barely keep her hands on the wheel to pull into the scenic overlook without taking the Lancia over the edge of the cliff. She killed the engine and bolted from the car

"Oh my god, oh my god! What have I done?"

She cried and paced and suddenly ran to the safety rail and vomited over the edge. But then her blood froze, and she thought her heart would stop when she heard a low moan from the passenger seat of her car.

She's dead! I know she's dead! There was no pulse.

Should she turn and look? She was afraid to, but she feared even more being caught unawares, so she whipped around and slammed against the guard rail, panting.

"Help me!" called a voice from the depth of the car. Nikki paled. Had her years of care-free living finally caught up with her? Had she lost her mind?

"Please help me!"

Nikki stumbled to the car and stared into a pair of frightened, almond-shaped eyes. The woman, very much alive, seemed to relax when she saw her, but then she began to struggle against the seat belt. Finally, Nikki came alive.

"Wait! Let me get that."

She reached through the window and unbuckled her. The woman winced and slumped forward.

"Why am I in this car? And why does my head feel like it's going to explode?"

"W...well...I'll g...get to that, but f...first I have to make sure you're ok...I thought you were d...dead."

"You put dead people in your car?"

Nikki shook her head. "Of c...course not. I just...I hit you and I c...couldn't find a pulse...and..." She knew she was incriminating herself, but she couldn't stop. "I panicked and put you in there until I could figure out what to do."

"At least you're honest."

Nikki nodded "To a fault. It gets me in a lot of trouble."

They studied each other for a few minutes. While the other woman appraised Nikki's classic hair style, her immaculate grooming and expensive clothing, Nikki took in the stranger's lack thereof. Tattered clothing, worn and dirty, bare feet, gaunt features and scruffy hair gave away her status as a homeless person. Nikki suddenly crimsoned with shame.

"I live right up the hill here. Let me get you to my house and I'll see if I can help you."

"And you are my...rescuer? ...captor? ...killer?"

"I'm sorry. Where are my manners? I am Nicola Portman. My friends call me Nikki."

"Portman? Like...the shoe people?"

"Yes, Frank Portman was my father."

"Well, I'll be doggoned! I've been kidnapped by the Shoe Princess."

Nikki winced. She hated that title. It brought home the emptiness of her pampered existence. And besides…"I'm not kidnapping you. I mean…not really. I'm just trying to help."

"You could have called 9-1-1."

She dropped her head. "About that…I'm really sorry. I'll make it up to you."

Despite growing up wealthy, Nikki had remained rather innocent. It never crossed her mind that this stranger might take advantage of her. "Can I just bring you to my place and see what I can do for you, Ms…?"

"It's Rosaleigh, but you can call me Rose."

"Well…Rose?"

"Let's go then. I'm not getting any better sitting here."

Nikki had never run anyone down before, so she didn't notice that Rose acted oddly for someone just hit by a car. She also hadn't had enough contact with homeless folks to realize that the subtle signs of depression and resignation, so common on the streets, were missing from her involuntary passenger. Rose seemed bright and alert and despite her skinniness and tattered appearance, she presented herself with an uncommon dignity.

Neither of them spoke much until Nikki pulled into her driveway and stopped at the wrought-iron gate. At the keypad, she punched in her personal code, which she changed weekly and the giant gate slid open almost without making a sound.

"You live behind walls," said Rose. "It looks like a prison."

Nikki frowned. "Wait until you get inside."

It was dark enough that the yard with its manicured lawn, its lush trees and shrubbery and its multi-colored flower splendor might have hidden in the shadows, but for the spotlights that illuminated here and there. Rosaleigh stared.

"I'll be doggoned! Somebody pinch me!"

Nikki smiled. Although she had a caretaker who did most of the hard work, she prided herself on planning and planting with taste and dedication. As the gate slid closed behind them, Rose turned and watched through the rear window.

"It's still a prison."

Nikki helped Rose out of the car and into the house and made her strip down to examine her for injuries. Rose's hip glowed purple with a giant bruise and her shoulder, skinned and angry red, burned like fire.

"I have stuff to fix that," said Nikki, shamefaced.

"What if I broke something? Or get a blood clot?"

Nikki sighed, picked up her cell phone and dialed a number. Rose watched her silently.

"Doc, how are you? Do you have a minute?" Nikki spoke into the phone rapidly, not giving her physician friend a chance to say no. "Hypothetically...if someone hits someone with a car – and I'm not saying I did – could they get a blood clot?"

"It's possible. Nikki...what happened? Did you...?"

"Hypothetically, Doc!"

"Nikki, a lot of things can happen when someone gets hit by a car. Would this hypothetical person need to go to an emergency room?"

"She's up and talking, but she's kind of bruised up….hypothetically."

"Well, she probably needs to be seen…"

"Can you make a house call? I don't want any publicity."

"It's after hours, Nikki. Have you been drinking?"

"That's the other thing. Can you just do me this one favor?"

Silence on the other side, while the minutes ticked away. Nikki bit her lip and held her breath. Dr. Perry wanted to go out with her but so far she had not agreed. Perhaps she would have to.

"Alright Nik, but just this once."

Once again, Nikki's legendary good luck prevailed. Rose had no injuries, beyond a few bruised ribs and skinned elbows. Handsome Dr. Perry watched Nikki over the rims of his glasses, as she fluttered around his patient.

"You know you owe me one," he said.

She sighed. "Alright, Doc. Lunch next week."

Dr. Perry hesitated, sensing her reluctance. But the man in him blotted out his better reason, and he said, "I'm free on Wednesday."

When she didn't respond, he let himself out. He would call her later on.

The two women shared a bottle of wine and some peanuts, and Nikki, with genuine interest, asked Rose for her story.

"Not much to tell," said Rose, "but explain to me instead why you are leading the doctor on."

"What makes you think I won't go out with him?"

"Oh, you will. That much I figured out by now. You'll go on one cordial date with the poor man, and then you'll let him down easy. Isn't that what you usually do?"

Nikki leaned forward, thunderstruck. "How do you know that?"

"I see it in your eyes. You're still waiting for Mr. Right."

Nikki sighed. She pulled her feet up on the couch and hugged a pillow. "I've been married six times. Which one of them do you suppose was Mr. Right?"

"Good gracious! Do you even look at them before you meet them at the altar?"

Nikki pouted. "That's not fair. I love them when I marry them. It just sort of fizzles out. At least I'm not sleeping around."

"No, you're just *marrying* around."

A furrow formed on Nikki's pretty forehead. She was too polite to snap at the other woman, but the warmth fled from her voice when she replied. "Just because I hit you with a car does not give you the right to criticize my lifestyle."

Rose chuckled. "I suppose if that doesn't, nothing does. But never mind. Let me tell you a story instead that may appeal to you, since you seem to be looking for a fairy tale."

Nikki relaxed. A good story over a fine glass of wine, what could beat that? "Once upon a time…?" she prompted.

Rose laughed. "No, this story starts another way. The prince I'm going to tell you about still lives."

"A prince?"

"Yes, he lives, but in exile. It was, however, not always so."

"Alright, don't keep me in suspense any longer."

"This is the story of a prince, now possibly in his middle years. He is an intelligent man, kind and gentle with a good heart. Yet, while a good hearted ruler is praised and welcomed in peaceful times, he cannot rule if a country is in uproar. And if power hungry generals make violent plans for takeover, he is ill prepared to back them down and restore order. Such it was with this ruler, Prince Xaoul. The coup was so well organized that the royal forces were beaten in the span of two days, and Xaoul barely escaped with his life. Tragically, his beloved wife, Zia, was killed during the skirmish, and he could not even return for the burial. He grieves to this day and is ridden with guilt.

"Xaoul escaped with only the clothes on his back, but his loyal subjects who smuggled him to safety, also transferred out his private assets, which were quite substantial and allowed Xaoul to purchase a large estate.

"Security issues and his deep, unrelenting grief made him shy of public appearances. He had a mansion built with many rooms and doors, each leading to the next room and each bolted with a different lock. At the center of this building, Xaoul lives to this day, barricaded away from the world with enough supplies to last decades. Although his countrymen have since overthrown the ambitious general, have rallied around him and are preparing for his return, he will not leave his mansion. He lives there, shut away from love or laughter, from friendship or pleasure, and mourns. There is only one who can enter, who was given the keys – one hundred of them – for safe keeping. And some day there may be another, a woman of extraordinary quality, whose compassion opens all doors and breaks down the walls around his lonely heart. Only then will he answer the pleas of his countrymen, return to his country and ascend the throne once again. And he will bring with him a princess to share his life and to rule his household."

Into the silence, Nikki said, "And then?"

"The end."

"The end? How can this be the end? It hasn't even happened yet."

Rose smiled and in her eyes stood a thousand secrets. "Well, that's where you come in."

"I beg your pardon?"

"You could become the woman who opens all doors."

"Rose, what are you talking about? This is a fairy tale!"

"Yes, it is. And it could be yours."

"Dr. Perry was wrong. You do have a concussion!"

Rose shook her head. "No, I'm fine. But you're obviously not the romantic I took you to be."

Nikki rose from the couch and gathered the empty wine bottle and glasses. "Perhaps we'd better call it a night then. I'll show you where you can sleep."

Nikki woke late the next day. Despite years of drinking, she still got hangovers and her energy flat-lined after a wild night. After two aspirin and a glass of water, she felt halfway prepared to face the day but not in the least ready to deal with her house guest. To her surprise, the guest room stood wide open, the bed was untouched, and a note was pinned to the bed coverlet.

Thank you for your hospitality. Please meet me today at noon at the shelter on the corner of Fifth Street and Central. It's important!
Rose

What could be so important that she had to drive back into town? Perhaps Rose had second thoughts and wanted some money. Perhaps she had better find out. She puttered around the house until her headache subsided and then called the doctor.

"It's Sunday morning. Why aren't you in church?" he teased her.

"Hangover. What's your excuse?"

"I had to work late. Some crazy lady made me make a house call."

"Oh, did she come to the door in a negligee and seduce you?"

He sighed. "No, but that would have been nice."

There was a pause, during which Dr. Perry's mood dampened. "How's our patient this morning?" he asked.

"She escaped. That's why I'm calling. She left me a note. I don't think she even touched the bed."

"Well, she's an adult. I suppose, she can leave whenever she wants to."

"I'm worried that she's not right in the head. She told me a fantastic story and left me a note to meet her at the shelter at noon."

"What kind of story?"

"Oh some fairy tale about a prince. Do you think she's dangerous?"

"I can't say for sure, but she seemed quite normal to me. A bit eccentric perhaps, but that comes from living on the streets."

"You think I should meet her then?"

"As long as you stay in a public area, why not? At least find out what she wants. She didn't steal anything did she?"

"No, everything is untouched."

"She's honest. That's nice to know. I'd say go meet her and let me know how it goes."

She had never been to the homeless shelter; there had been no occasion. As she approached the tall, ugly building, she thought she might volunteer there, if only it didn't look so much like a jail. She entered hesitantly, unsure if she would be admitted or if the big, burly looking security guard would bar her way.

"I'm looking for a friend," she said. "Her name is Rose."

The security guard looked over her trim figure appreciatively. "I'm sorry Ma'am, I can't give out the names of our residents."

"She's expecting me." Nikki showed him the note.

"If you tell me your name, perhaps I can ask around."

"I'm Nicola Portman. Nikki for short."

The guard's face brightened. "Wait here. I think I can help you."

He returned with a package and handed it to Nikki. Her name was scrawled in capital letters across the wrapper. The package weighed a couple of pounds, although it was quite small.

"Rose checked out a couple of days ago. She left this for you before she took off."

Nikki shook her head. "That can't be. I only just met her last night."

"Are you sure? She specifically said to give you this."

"So she didn't come here last night? How strange!"

"We haven't seen her since Friday."

Nikki took the package to her car and opened it with trembling fingers. She was more than a little spooked by the peculiar mixed up chronology. Inside, she found a note and a bundle of keys. She stared. There had to be dozens of them! She unfolded the note and read.

Dear Nikki,
Sometimes, we stand at a crossroads and must make a decision on which way our lives are to continue. If we go one way, all will be familiar. We will continue to have the same experiences, meet the same kinds of people, make the same mistakes. However, if we find the courage to go the other way, we will leave our comfort zone and travel a new path. If we take the risk to change, everything will become new and fresh, in an exciting, but sometimes dangerous way. You have in your hands the keys to the castle. They will open all doors and pave the way to a possible future. If you dare, you can free a captive soul and live the fairy tale. You showered me with kindness. Let me repay you in this way.
The map to the castle is on the back. Your prince is waiting…
Sincerely, Rose

One hundred keys! Of course. She tried to think past the fog in her head and remember Rose's story. It had sounded so fantastic last night.

"If she really left this on Friday and I only met her last night, there must be some strange magic involved." Nikki realized she was talking to herself and looked up quickly to make sure nobody had noticed.

The map seemed simple enough. The town closest to the mansion lay about an hour's drive away. Suddenly, Nikki was wide awake. The mystery struck her like a thunderbolt and she fought to catch her breath. She had a full tank of gas and no obligations. What was to keep her from taking a look?

The sun already burned brightly overhead when Nikki pulled her Lancia into the park road that led to the mansion atop a hill. The grass had recently been mowed. Although an adventurous spirit tingled up and down her back, Nikki remained wary of receiving a frosty welcome. After all, she was trespassing.

Of course, the gate was locked. The prince did not want company. She sat unmoving in the Lancia for a few long minutes, before hesitantly picking up the giant, heavy bundle of keys.

"Which one do I use?" she murmured. "They all look alike."

She got lucky. The fifth key opened the gate. For a moment, she remained breathless. Her voice rang out jubilantly in the midmorning silence.

"It's real! The story and all. It's really real!"

She locked the gate from the inside and left the key in the lock, hoping no one would remove it. This would enable her to leave easily and give her one less key to worry about. Still, it might take hours, even days, to open ninety-nine more doors. Did she really want to attempt it?

Perhaps it was the fairy tale that drove her on, the promise of everlasting love with a man, deserving of it. Perhaps it was only her craving for the unusual, her taste for adventure that made her climb back into the Lancia and speed up the hill to the mansion.

The house stood several stories tall and did not appear to have any windows. The moment she opened the entry portal and stepped inside, time lost all meaning. She felt as if she had always been in this house, turning keys, unlocking and locking giant oak doors. The walls had a forever quality, and the air smelled musty and medieval. Each room she entered seemed darker and more forbidding yet drew her in with an irresistible pull.

Many doors later, she still plodded on. Hunger churned in her empty stomach, her feet hurt in thin-soled flats, her eyes burned, and her hands shook as she turned key after key after key. Some doors opened on a stairway, others revealed corridors, others still gave way to wide, echoing halls. Painstakingly, she re-locked the doors and left the keys behind. Smaller and smaller grew her bundle of keys, yet it seemed to weigh more heavily in her tired hands.

I should go back and get something to eat and drink.

But, she plodded on, as if life had but one single purpose: to free the captive prince from his self-assumed prison. Not once did she stop to question the sanity of her actions.

The last few rooms she crossed on hands and knees. Weakness shook her, and she chilled in the cool, stale air. She wept, from exhaustion, but also because the drama of the moment had seized her and transformed her into a suffering heroine. She was no longer Nikki the Shoe Princess, but a valiant woman, younger than her years, who fought for love and justice and believed in magic.

She all but fell into the prince's chambers. The door had not given easily, and for a while, she had wondered if another key might be blocking the lock from inside. It took all her strength to push the door open, and she collapsed at the feet of a middle aged man of average height, but regal bearing, who looked down at her with large, almond shaped eyes.

"Are you the one?" His melodious voice carried easily through the spacious hall, although he had spoken quietly.

"Yes," she wept. Summoning all her strength and all her courage, she lifted her head and looked at him. And fainted.

When she came to, she rested on a brocaded sofa, pillows tucked all around her. The prince sat across from her and watched her with concerned eyes. He handed her a glass of water, from which she drank in deep, thirsty draughts.

"She never told you how hard it would be, did she?"

"Who?"

"My mother, of course. Rosaleigh, the former queen."

"Rose!" Nikki's eyes widened and she nodded thoughtfully. He had the same eyes, the same build. It had to be.

He smiled and it made him look handsome in an unconventional way. Finely chiseled cheek bones framed a smooth face. A narrow nose rose steeply over full lips. A gold tooth gleamed between them, bearing the symbols of moon and star. She noticed the same symbol on a ring on his right hand.

"I am Xaoul, the exiled prince. Have you come to return me to my people?"

"I don't know. I was given the keys."

He nodded. "You are the one then."

They spoke at length, about Rose, about Nikki's life, about Xaoul's banishment. After a while, their hands found each other and much later their lips. She lay in his arms, when she finally asked him, "Where is your country? Rose never told me."

"It's not so much a matter of where as a matter of when and maybe how."

She searched his exotic features, his slight figure which nevertheless glowed with health and vigor and sighed. "You are not of this world, are you?"

"No," said the prince.

For a long time, Nikki thought quietly of the implications. In her mind, she saw her beautiful home on the hillside, with its lush, green garden and its spectacular view. She thought of her brothers who excluded her from the family business and paid her lavishly to stay out of the way. She remembered her friends and the men in her life, whom she had loved and left. If Xaoul asked her, would she be able to leave it all behind and travel with him?

Just then, the prince took both her hands in his well manicured ones. With pale lips and deeply serious eyes, he said, "Nikki, I feel as though I should warn you. I'm not an easy man to live with, but I am kind and caring. I believe that you are the one my mother sent me, the one fate has chosen for me. As I am gathering my courage to return to my country, I am asking you to find yours. If you go with me, you can never come back. I will be crowned king, and I wish to make you my queen."

Nikki stared at her hands, especially her left, ring-less one. Six husbands, six bitter disappointments, six fairy tale weddings followed by six whirlwind divorces. Could she risk it one more time?

"What if I'm not happy with you or in your kingdom?"

"I cannot answer that. Remember though that in every fairy tale, king and queen live happily ever after."

She looked up and studied the face of the man who was to be her husband and her king. Secretly, she compared him to Doc and to some of the other men who were clamoring to date her. He won, hands down. His exotic features and proud bearing outshone them all. And just then, he dropped to one knee before her and looked up at her earnestly.

"Marry me!" he said. "Marry me and go with me tonight."

"What about my things? I'll need clothes...shoes..."

"There is no time. We must go quickly. The portal is open only a short time."

"How will we travel?"

"You came in a car, did you not?"

Nikki nodded. "My Lancia stands outside in the court yard."

"We will need it to travel, but once at the portal, we will leave it behind."

He sounded so sincere, that Nikki never once doubted his truthfulness. Together, they loaded Xaoul's boxes of court papers and decrees and locked up the mansion. Like she often did, when traveling with a man, she handed Xaoul the keys to the Lancia, but he shook his head.

"I don't drive anything that doesn't have a horse in front of it."

Nikki smiled and cranked the Lancia, revving up the engine. She would miss this car. She shifted into first gear and rolled away slowly, giving the engine time to warm up before picking up speed.

Doc was called to the scene because it was known that he and Nikki had been friends, although there was no body to identify. The Lancia had flipped at least twice, before landing upside down in a ditch. The impact had crushed the light sports car, ripped off the doors and broken loose the rear axle. Scrap metal lay scattered over both sides of the road. Broken glass crunched under the feet of the investigating officers. Despite evidence that another person had ridden in the car with her, neither his body nor Nikki's were ever found.

Doc left the scene of the accident in tears. It took a couple of hours, before he regained enough composure to begin calling Nikki's friends and relatives.

He attended the memorial service, a dark, silent figure in black. His grief equaled that of her brothers and of her nearest friends. Would it have helped them all to know that the Shoe Princess had indeed become a real princess and lived happily ever after?

The Kiss That Changed The World

A small, pudgy boy wanders into the dimly lit music room. His feet smack the stone floor smartly, and his steps echo in the shadows.

He looks over his shoulder for Nannerl, his sister, but she has not followed him. A gleam of independence lights his dark, expressive eyes. It is rare that he finds himself so alone.

It may surprise you to see such a small boy in velvet breeches and a silk waistcoat, but his short stature is misleading. He aged out of dresses and leading strings at least two years ago. His stubby feet, shod in high heel buckle shoes, move with purpose. He is drawn to the black shiny thing by the window: The Pianoforte.

He was only three when he began to watch Nannerl during her lessons. Intrigued by the gleaming ivories, he reached out his hand once in a while. With two tiny toddler hands, he pushed keys until a chord pleased him. Then, he giggled when his father smiled.

Time and work has passed since those carefree days. Father is a patient teacher, but stern. And Wolfgang doesn't like displeasing the Kapellmeister. But today, Father is not here, so the boy uncovers the ivories eagerly. This is his time. He can play any melody he likes.

When he strikes the first chord, he feels a presence in the room. His head snaps around, but he sees no one. A gentle touch breezes over his bare hand. Then, a voice, light and sweet, whispers in his ear.

"Wolfgang," says the voice. "Do you want to make great music?"

The boy huddles. He dares not move nor speak. He thinks of Fräulein Anna next door, who lost her mind from hearing voices.

"Wolfgang. Do not fear me. I am here to help you."

"You can't," he says, then stops. He cannot be seen talking to a ghost.

"I am not what you think," whispers the voice. It sounds like birds trilling or bells ringing. It seems to him the sweetest sound he ever heard.

"Who are you then? And what do you want of me?"

Laughter, like delicate glass breaking into a thousand tiny shards.

"Let me kiss you, child, and you shall make the greatest music ever heard on earth!"

He hesitates. No young boy wants kisses from a ghost. He turns sideways a bit. "Are you a woman?"

More laughter and another feather-light touch on his hand. "I am a Muse."

He turns a little more, toward the source of the sweet voice. "A Muse? And you can help me make great music?"

She caresses his hair, which, still soft, falls past his ears in golden waves. "I can, Wolfgang. It is my destiny – and yours."

"Well then," says the boy. "Help me reach my destiny. Let my father be proud of me, as he is of my sister."

"Yes," says the voice. And the sweetest touch warms the boy's young face, grazes his lips and burns like fire in his soul. Only a moment, and it is over. The voice is gone, and the room is empty once again, but for a small boy sitting at a piano.

Wolfgang Amadeus Mozart's fingers reach for the ivory keys and strike a chord. A melody sings out. With eyes alight and breathless, he charms notes from his instrument and smiles. In his mind, a score of music forms. He plays it twice from beginning to end before he runs for paper and pencils. With impatient fingers, he writes: notes and pauses, chords and phrases, in just minutes. Above the score, he writes the name of his piece. He calls it *Andante*.

Inn And Out

Sarai's story:

"There's your favorite customer, Sarai," teased the innkeeper and pointed out the kitchen window. "It's the third time this week. Reckon it's our ale he's after?"

"Hush Papa! He'll hear you!"

"He won't. Not with all the ruckus his friends are making out there, knocking snow off their boots."

"Thank the stars!" Sarai felt a familiar flush crawl up her neck and redden her ears.

"As long as he keeps bringing his friends, and as long as they pay their tab at the end of the night, he can woo you all he wants."

"It's not like that, Papa. He's really nice."

A cold draft chilled her heated face. She heard voices in the tavern and the closing of a heavy door. Patrons rustled out of furred winter coats and called greetings. Chairs scraped across the wooden floor.

"I guess you'd better go see about them."

"Papa, I'm chopping vegetables. Can't you go?"

The innkeeper chuckled. "No, I don't think the wizard is here on my behalf. He'd be mighty disappointed to see my scruffy face."

Sarai sighed and wiped her hands on her apron. She picked up pad and paper and stepped into the dining room, smiling.

"Good evening folks! Glad you could make it in this horrible weather!"

The patrons, the wizard's usual collection of odd characters, returned her greeting with varying degrees of affability. The tavern, which had been nearly empty before, suddenly felt full.

"What can I get for you good folks?"

After a short discussion, they settled on wine, which pleased her. Not many could afford it these days. Most settled for the cheaper ale.

"We'll be serving rabbit stew in about an hour or so, and I made fresh bread this morning. Will you be wanting to eat?"

"Sure, bring it on!" said the miller, patting his ample belly. Nobody in the wizard's party worried about cost.

Sarai studied her patrons under lowered lashes while she loaded a tray with goblets, flatware and bowls.

Leah sat next to the miller, her husband. She was the friendlier of the two. The portly pair had produced a house full of boys, some of them grown now. One of the boys had cornered Sarai in the cellar one day and tried to cop a feel. She had thrown the cider jug at him and smashed his shoulder with it, dousing him with the contents. Her father, hearing the commotion had stepped into the cellar with a cudgel in hand, counting to ten. The boy managed to dodge out the door at 'eight.' Nobody told the miller but the boy left her alone after that, and Leah brought her some fine cake flour the next morning, free of charge.

"Need some help, Miss Sarai?" called Pan, the Duke's horseman. "We're getting a little thirsty here."

Sarai blushed. "I'm sorry. I'm coming."

Pan grinned broadly and patted her arm while she distributed the goblets on the table. His silver hair flowed down his back to his waist. His face disappeared under a gray mustache and beard, the latter almost as long as the hair on his head. Over the hairiness, a pair of eyes sparkled, mirth dancing in their corners.

"There, there. No harm done. I'm sure Cameron wouldn't mind helping you carry the wine from the cellar."

Cameron…the wizard. She had managed to avoid looking at him so far, but the intensity of his gaze burned on her face now.

"I…I can manage…thank you," she stuttered, turning crimson.

She fled from the room but not before noticing the wizard's smile, the light in his eyes, or the two ladies who flanked him closely, as though they were in competition over who could be nearest him.

She knew the one, garishly made up and dressed. An actress from the theater, forever trying to get her hands on the handsome mage. But the other?

She filled two stone jugs with their best wine. She would have to carry them one by one up the stairs. She almost regretted rejecting the wizard's help. But what would she do alone with him in the cellar?

She climbed the stairs, chastising herself for her wayward thoughts. The wizard was a gentleman, and she only an innkeeper's daughter. And what signs had he given her that he would be even slightly interested? She blushed again. There had been some.

The lady at his right smiled when Sarai brought the wine. Full lips parted to reveal sparkling white teeth. Black tresses tumbled down past her shoulders and gleamed in the candle light, casting shadows on smooth, alabaster skin. A pretty lady indeed. Who was she?

"Tip the girl," she said, and Cameron conjured a coin from the air and gave it to Sarai. It was a gold coin - the wizard tipped heavy.

Without taking his eyes off her, he conjured a sweetly scented white flower and placed it gently in her hair. The lady at his right stopped smiling.

Sarai escaped to the kitchen to help her father with the stew. He looked up from the pot he was stirring and grinned.

"What was all that about?"

Sarai didn't answer but twirled the coin in her hand. Laughter floated from the tavern, and she frowned. Were they laughing at her expense?

When the stew was done, she ladled it into a large bowl and carried it to the table. The patrons of the inn knew to serve themselves. The pretty lady watched Sarai with hard eyes.

Sarai returned with a basket of freshly sliced bread. The lady still glared at her, so she set the bread right in front of the wizard, fluttered her eyes and smiled.

"I baked it with extra butter today."

He winked at her and reached for the bread but the lady was faster. She knocked her goblet over and spilled her wine all over the fresh bread.

"Oh how clumsy of me! Now it's all ruined. Now we'll need more bread and more wine."

Sarai flushed and bit her lip. She snatched the dripping basket from the table and tried to sop up the wine with her apron. Cameron leaped up to help her but the lady had latched on to his arm and pulled him back to his seat.

"Careful dear man, we don't want to knock over the soup as well."

Sarai dumped the wet basket into the sink and hurried to slice more bread.

If she has to be ugly toward me, she must see me as a threat! The thought made her giddy.

Pan took the bread from her and handed her the empty pitchers, his eyes filled with understanding. She scurried to the cellar.

A tingle crawled up her back when she turned off the tap. She knew the feeling. There was someone else in the cellar. She spun around to a soft voice speaking.

"I apologize for my companion's mishap," said the wizard.

She frowned. "That was no mishap."

"I know. But I apologize just the same."

Silence fell between them, long enough to get uncomfortable. Sarai looked over the wizard's shoulder.

"She won't follow me if that's what you're thinking."

"Oh? How…"

"A man has to go to the privy sometimes."

"This is not the privy."

"I know."

The wizard leaned in the doorway with arms crossed. His handsome face hid in shadows but his eyes sparkled. His voice carried, though it was soft as silk and if she closed her eyes, she could feel his magic. His lips parted and the tip of his tongue appeared between them, lingered, teased. He smiled.

"So…what…"

"Do.I want with you?"

"Yes," she said, surprised at how breathless she was.

He moved toward her then, youthful arms snaked around her, pulling her close. Long, slender fingers crept up her back and buried in her hair. A supple body, hard in the loins pressed against hers. She lifted her face and his lips found hers. She'd been kissed before but never by a mage.

It hurt. It made her head pound and her skin burn. Her bones felt as though they would break, and pain in her gut made her want to double over. Something reached into her chest and squeezed her heart, kept squeezing until she was about to faint. She tore away from him and screamed, gasping for air.

From out of the chaos, a woman's voice called, "Cameron, for Pete's sake! Let her go!"

Sarai came to on the cellar floor. Above her, the wizard and the lady glared at each other. The wine pitchers had burst and wine ran across the floor. In the doorway stood her father, cudgel in hand, looking from one to the other.

"What in blazes is going on here?"

"Papa," she whimpered. "I fell and hit my head but I'm alright now. Don't worry."

"You sure, honey?"

"Yes, Papa."

Sarai rose and began to pick up broken pieces of the wine jars.

"Leave it, honey. I'll clean up here. Go back up and see to the guests."

"Yes, Papa."

Out of sight of her father, the lady laid a silk gloved hand on her arm. Her voice was warm with concern.

"I'm sorry for the trouble we caused. We'll be leaving in a minute. Please forgive us." Then, sharper, "Cameron, your purse – please!"

Without a word, the wizard handed her a purse full of coin, and she pressed it into the girl's hand.

"Half for the trouble and the other half for your silence."

Sarai nodded. There was nothing else left to say.

Nina's story:

Nina stomped her feet to knock snow off her boots. Anxious to get into the warm tavern, she pushed past the miller and his wife and opened the door. The smell of stew and fresh yeast bread wafted out. Her small company entered and peeled out of heavy winter coats. The millers squeezed behind the large round table, and the rest of them settled around it, she, next to her wizard.

This was the first time she had come with him to this particular tavern. She wasn't sure why she felt the need to tag along this time. It was just a vague feeling.

The friendly waitress brought an excellent wine, better than she would have expected in such a small tavern. And the girl endured some good natured ribbing from the ever witty Pan.

"Tip the girl," she told Cameron, and he conjured a coin and gave it to the waitress. Nina smiled.

But then, Cameron conjured a flower and set it in the waitress' hair, and Nina caught the sudden energy between the two of them.

Oh no, not again!

"Uh-oh, Cam, you're in the doghouse!" teased Pan. Everyone laughed but Nina.

When the girl brought the stew, Nina watched her. Tension built in the back of her neck. A sense of foreboding began to throb in her temples. And then the girl flirted openly with the wizard. Nina's sensitive nature felt the magic swirl in the room. She'd been with the wizard long enough to distinguish the pattern. She sensed danger.

She spilled her wine to break the spell. She didn't mean to be unkind toward the girl but she needed to act quickly. She clung to Cameron while Pan helped the embarrassed waitress.

After a few minutes, the wizard rose to his feet. Nina took his hand.

"Where are you going?"

"To get rid of this wine. Surely you don't want to come with me to the privy?"

The others looked at her strangely. She lowered her eyes and let go of his hand. Under her lashes, she watched whither he went, not trusting him even one damn bit.

She cast a spell of her own, so she could slip away unseen and follow him, follow the scent of his magic.

She came almost too late. The girl in his arms was gasping, life almost squeezed from her heart. Nina raised all her power and knocked him in the head with it, making him release his grip. The girl screamed.

"Cameron, for Pete's sake, let her go!"

He spun around and glared at her. "What'd you follow me for?"

"Have you forgotten already what happened last time? I like this town. I don't want to have to run away again just because you can't control yourself around these young girls. I came just in time or you'd have killed her."

His head dropped. The madness went out of his eyes. He took in the mess he'd made. Behind him, the innkeeper appeared in the doorway with a cudgel. Nina willed the girl to speak.

"I fell and hit my head but I'm alright now."

The girl looked dazed and frightened. Nina felt only compassion. Out of sight of her father, she placed a gentle hand on the young woman's arm.

"I'm sorry for the trouble we caused. We'll be leaving in a minute. Please forgive us." Then, sharper, "Cameron, your purse - please!"

Without a word, the wizard handed her a purse full of coin, and she pressed it into Sarai's hand.

"Half for the trouble and the other half for your silence."

To her relief, the girl only nodded.

Cameron's story:

She smells so sweet. I can detect her scent from across the room. I could sniff her out in a crowd, I think. I just want to be near her.

The wizard let his gaze rest for a moment on the young girl's face. He traced the roundness of her cheek, the slope of her shoulders, the gentle swell of her breasts. The plainness of her young face did not put him off and neither did her lack of adornments or her lack of status. He had fought to control his feelings but found himself coming back to her tavern again and again, drawn by her simple charm.

It was different with Nina. She was a beautiful companion but she had her own magic, which gave their lovemaking a crisper, more brittle flavor and left him longing for the innocents, the common ones, those without magic.

Sarai avoided his eyes, but he saw her blush, and heat from reddened cheeks increased the natural perfume of her skin.

"I'm sure Cameron wouldn't mind helping you carry the wine from the cellar." Pan said, making her stutter.

Don't think I haven't considered it, old man!

Would she have him? Her reserved manner left him guessing. He needed a sign. She blushed again, when he placed a flower behind her ear. The softness of her hair made his hand tremble. He ached from wanting her.

Her lashes fluttered, and she smiled just for him, come-hither in her eyes. His sign!

And then, Nina spilled the wine, her back stiff, and her jaw set hard in anger.

He found Sarai in the cellar. Never one to use force, he approached gently. When he heard a hopeful tremor in her voice, he took her in his arms. Her heady scent washed over him, and his loins hardened against her. Magic swirled through the cellar.

He meant to be tender, but in the thrill of her embrace he lost his head and control of his magic. She raised her head, and their lips met. With the kiss, all his power broke free, searing with pain the young girl in his arms.

"Cameron, for Pete's sake, let her go!"

Nina! Why had she followed him?

"I came just in time or you'd have killed her."

Cameron dropped his head. It was Nina – and always Nina – who righted his wrongs. His purse, heavy with gold once again paid for his weakness, once again bought someone's silence.

Sarai accepted his money without a word.

Demon Lover

Salika's breath quickened as she hastened along the narrow path. She scarcely noticed the shadows which danced under the ancient elm trees. Hope drew her deeper and deeper into the coolness of the grove. Night would fall soon. She must hurry.

She grumbled her anger as she ran. Her mother, always in a crisis, always needing her help, had delayed her. Now she feared that he would not be there. That he would discard her for a more deserving woman. Perhaps for one of those annoying females she dealt with daily at the beauty shop.

She veered from the path and scrambled up a steep hillside, covered in brambles which scratched her legs and made her stumble. She cursed quietly, but climbed on. He was worth a little pain. If only she were not too late!

She reached the clearing just as the last light faded from the trees. Her throat ached and burned, and her breath rushed hard in and out of tortured lungs. She fell to her knees, wheezing.

Please be here! Please!

Strong arms snaked around her huddled form and gathered her up easily. She shivered when his heat singed her skin. A gasp of relief escaped her. He was here! She felt him by her ear, and then he bit her. And she wept with remorse for making him wait.

"I almost left," he said, his voice low and dark. "There are others who yearn for me."

"I yearn," she cried out, using the unfamiliar word awkwardly. "Please don't leave me!"

The scent of sulfur that always clung to him flooded her senses. She had long since lost her free will to it. She turned and yielded, losing herself in his radiant eyes and in the agony which followed.

She was not built to accommodate a demon, but he willed her to surrender. He tied her hands with hair from his back and singed her body with his touch. Pleasure and pain mingled in her senses until she could no longer tell the difference. She wept and sighed, while he used her body and worked his dark magic on her. Stars glistened in her eyes and fire burned in her heart and belly when he devoured her spirit, again and again.

When he withdrew from her, hours later, satisfied, but hardly gentled, she fell spent at his feet. She had wept until he burned up her tears, moaned until he broke down her voice. Her skin blistered and swelled where he had seized her, bruised to the bone. No human would ever touch her this way. None ever could. He looked down where she lay, all used up and burned out. She had nothing left to give; it was time to move on.

First rays of daylight crept through the thicket, and he faded into the shadows quietly. Salika slept on the forest floor until the sun stood at high noon. She felt tired and old, but her spirit still soared from the night's encounter. Chosen among humans, she alone could boast of a demon lover's attentions. Others could only envy her.

That was the last time she saw the demon. Although she went back to the grove night after night, he never returned for her. While she lost her mind with unrequited desire, somewhere else a woman writhed and moaned under his fiery touch.

When she slit her wrists, her family suddenly took notice. The doctors saved her reluctant life seconds before it faded and kept her in a psychiatric ward for observation. She is there to this day. She refuses to speak to anyone in or out of the hospital, but she holds hour-long conversations with imaginary ghosts at night. From time to time, when she feels unobserved, she opens her suitcase and takes out the dress she wore on that last, significant night. She holds it to her face and draws the air in sharply. She smiles then and only then. The dress is old and faded, but it holds his memory. And it smells of sulfur still today.

A Rose Is Just A Rose

The witch had thought the rose hedge to be impenetrable. She had chosen a variety with the most thorns and largest flowers. All around the castle she planted them, no more than two feet apart, in staggered formation to form a wall six feet thick. Behind the wall slept the child she had not been able to kill despite trying. It took the combined power of a twelve witch coven to bend her curse and soften it. A kiss would wake her and her household as well. A kiss would undo all her spelling and cursing. So she grew the roses to keep out potential kissers. It was the best she could do.

She grew the roses to keep rescuers out but also to keep herself from compulsively looking at the lovely child. It did her no good to see the princess. Her beauty cut deeply into the heart of the ugly witch. Oh how she hated that girl! She, herself had never possessed beauty. Her face did not inspire poetry, and her form did not cause men to knock at her door or sing under her window. And yet she, too, was of the royal blood, in direct line of succession for the throne but unloved and unwanted.

Decades later, roses twined thickly around the old castle, climbing over walls and towers until nary a glimpse of marble caught the eye. They bloomed all summer and filled the air with the sweetest fragrance. The castle was long forgotten, and none guessed what hid behind all that beauty

The witch tended her roses as any good gardener would, pruning and fertilizing, dusting and watering. People came from far to admire the stunning display.

From time to time, an adventurous youth would try to squeeze through the hedge to see what was beyond but the roses pricked him, ripped his clothes and sent him away naked and bleeding. The witch hid behind a tree and snickered.

Behind the wall of roses also slumbered the twelve of the coven who had been at the castle at the time of the hexing. With the coven asleep, the lone witch's powers waned until it took all her might just to maintain the roses. And so she poured herself into that task as a mother would pour herself into the task of raising a beloved child, and in her devotion she created something beautiful, on the walls of the castle as well as in her heart.

One morning, a young wanderer came to the enchanted castle. He was a man full of dreams and song, and when he saw the roses, he stopped to admire. But instead of just standing there or trying to pick a bloom or push through the vines, the young man sat below one of the rose bushes, pulled a small notebook from his pack and began to write a sonnet. From time to time, he murmured a line of words so beautiful, it touched the witch's heart. The rose bush, below which he sat, also began to take notice, bending its vines to look over the poet's shoulders and read his lovely words. When shadows darkened his page, the youth looked up, but he didn't startle at being embraced by thorny vines. He smiled and closed his eyes and breathed the intoxicating fragrance. His heart soared, and his words became music, and as he raised his voice in song, the roses caressed his face, and the vines parted to show him what lay beyond the wall of green.

Still singing, he rose and pressed through the rose bush, which carefully hid its thorns from him. At last, he reached the wall of the castle and laid his hands on pure white marble. Outside the hedge, stood the witch, frozen with shock.

The poet sang his way along the castle wall, but when the witch tried to follow, the vines blocked her. In her anger, she snatched up a stick and beat the hedge with it until roses fell broken to the ground. Then she fell to her knees and wept, clutching handfuls of crushed blooms to her heart.

When the young man reached the castle gate, it opened, and when he stepped inside to see the princess asleep at the spinning wheel, his heart opened as well. Still singing, he bent over her and kissed her, and she woke and smiled when she heard his song. She reached for him, and he took her hand to aid her to her feet. He kissed her again.

Gradually, the rest of the household rose from slumber. They all stared at the young man whose voice echoed from the castle walls. But when they saw their princess alive and well and in his arms, they surrounded the couple and cheered. The coven of twelve, newly awakened stood by and smiled.

Outside the castle walls, the witch slit her own throat with thorny vines ripped from the savaged rose hedge. In an act of love and grief, sweet, fragrant rose petals floated down and covered her like a red velvet blanket.

Heartsmith

Millegran wiped his sweaty forehead and dropped the tongs on a steel table, beside the cooling axe. He stepped away from the fire toward the door of the smithy, where fresh morning air soothed fire-flushed skin on his bare chest. For a moment, the thought crossed his mind to go back inside, take a freshly forged blade and slash his own throat with it, but then his courage left him, and he only leaned against the door frame and closed his eyes.

He had labored all night. Piece by piece, he had forged and hammered, heated and cooled. His arms ached from wielding heavy tools, and his legs trembled from treading the massive twin bellows. The vat, which had held a hundred gallons of cold water to harden the steel, now sent billows of steam into the air.

Millegran's chest heaved. He struggled to breathe after a night in the sweltering smithy, and his lungs burned. He lumbered over to a well, a few feet from the smoke-blackened hut and lowered the bucket. He bent over the well and stared into its depth, daring himself to jump. He shook his head sadly and drew water, from which he first drank his fill, before pouring the rest over his head and shoulders.

The master would be pleased. Millegran had completed all orders, and every tool showed perfect workmanship. Now he had only to collect his wages and go home, where he could sink into merciful sleep and forgetfulness.

He heard a step on the narrow path and looked up.Yet, it was not the master, who ascended toward the smithy, but a darker fellow, with a hat and cloak the color of midnight and boots heavy enough to shoe a soldier's feet. Millegran scowled. Hospitality demanded that he offer the man food and drink, but he was too tired for it. Where was the master?

"A good morning to you, young fellow," the stranger called, when he reached the gate. His voice, bright and cheery, contrasted with his dark appearance. "You must be the blacksmith, the one they call the Halfling?"

Millegran nodded. "I am, although I loathe the name."

The stranger laughed. His face crinkled into tiny lines with deeper crow's feet around the eyes. "My apologies! What may I call you then?"

Millegran stepped forward. "Millegran's the name. And you are…?"

"I am Rizzo. Although I think my name has little to do with anything." He extended a heavy brown hand and Millegran grasped it. The stranger gripped with surprising strength. "It's been a long walk. I could use a drink."

"I have only water to offer you…and some stale bread from last night." He lied, hoping to discourage Rizzo from getting too comfortable. There was ham and cheese aplenty in the back of the smithy. "The master is not here yet," he said then.

"It is you I've come to see."

A hope so bright it could have blinded the sun leapt up in Millegran's lonely heart. As if she had left only yesterday, he remembered once again the smile of his lovely wife, her lithe, tall form and the gentle sing-song of her human voice.

"You bring me word of Rona!"

The stranger shook his head. "I'm sorry. I do not."

Millegran closed his eyes, so Rizzo would not see the abyss within them, as he plunged into sorrow once again. He gripped the edge of the well with hard fists, and the mortar beneath them crumbled. When he spoke again, his voice choked with emotion.

"What is it you want with me then?"

"Let me drink first, and I'll tell you."

Millegran drew water and watched, while the stranger drank in large, quick gulps. Up close, he didn't look quite as dark, but tall of build with strong arms and fire-scarred, heavily calloused hands.

"You're a blacksmith as well!"

"I was once. I still am, in a manner of speaking."

"If you are looking for work, you have to wait for the master. I don't do the hiring."

"I'm not for hire, but I might be able to help you."

Millegran stared. Did the stranger aim to take him away from his smithy, where he had spent his learning years? He couldn't' leave yet. The master wouldn't allow it.

"I still have a year to go at least. My master has refused me the journeyman papers."

"As he will continue to refuse them, as long as you agree to labor for him."

Millegran sighed. Rizzo echoed his own thoughts. It was a way for a master to extract more work from a former apprentice. And Millegran, being taller and broader than any dwarfs and looking to forget his sorrows, worked twice as hard as any other.

"There may be some beer in the smithy and a bite to eat - if you want to step inside."

Rizzo nodded. Like Millegran, he had to stoop through the doorway, but once inside, the smithy was built generously enough for both men to stand. A look at the tidy workplace and the carefully crafted tools and blades seemed to satisfy him greatly, and he smiled when he sat with Millegran to eat and talk.

Rizzo waited in the back of the smithy until the master appeared to inspect the night's workmanship and give the smith his pay. It wasn't much, what the master handed out – it never was – but it fed Millegran and kept him in liquor.

"Stop by later to see if we've taken in any new work," he said, as always. If they didn't, Millegran, accustomed to staying up, spent his nights drinking.

On the way to his house, Millegran passed by the inn. The innkeeper stood on his front steps, admiring the morning.

"Millegran, did you get paid today? You owe me a tab from last week."

"I'll catch you later. I have to sleep first."

The innkeeper nodded. "Make sure you bring money tonight or my daughter won't serve you anything."

Millegran shrugged. He disliked the innkeeper's brash daughter, who sat by him uninvited when he tried to drink away his sadness. Last time she had reached under the table to stroke the bulge in his pants and he had threatened to break her hand.

His house looked like all the other houses in the village, but with a taller doorway, allowing Millegran to walk in upright. He slung the heavy wooden shoes from his feet and fell on the bed with his trousers on. Minutes later, fatigue and a swig from a brandy bottle drugged him into a deep, dreamless sleep.

He woke from the afternoon heat. Cotton-mouthed, he craved water, but picked up instead a half-empty beer bottle and drank down the warm brew. He almost gagged on it and shook himself. His limbs still ached, but he rose and ambled outside to the well, where he drew water and drank deeply. He filled another bucket and stripped down to wash. He knew the innkeeper's daughter would be watching, but he didn't care. He would be gone in an hour.

It didn't take long to pack his few belongings. His work pants he left behind. The forge fire had burned holes in them, large enough to put a fist through. He put on a clean pair and packed two more, a shirt, a cloak, and a blanket. Following Rizzo's advice, he added a tin cup and plate, a spoon and a whetstone for his hunting knife. He tied the bundle and strapped his wooden shoes to it. He would walk barefoot for a while. His knife, he lashed to his side and stuffed flint and steel into his trouser pocket. He filled a canteen at the well and tied it to his belt.

He wished for coffee to clear his head, but he couldn't stop at the inn or the innkeeper would take his money, and he needed it for the journey. He took one last look at the village. There was nothing to keep him there.

He didn't want to attract attention, so he walked to the back of his hut and began ascending toward the watch tower. No breeze stirred the hot afternoon air, and Millegran welcomed the shade of the dense pine wood above the village. He circled the town and doubled back to the creek where Rizzo sat in the shade and smoked. His face brightened when he saw Millegran.

"I was afraid you had changed your mind."

"I took the long way to avoid questions."

Rizzo nodded and handed him a parchment. "Your travel papers. It says here that I purchased you fair and square from your master, and that you're to be my apprentice until I have taught you what you've come to learn. Once you are finished learning, I will make you a Journeyman. No repayment needed."

"I still don't know why you are doing this."

The other man grew solemn. "I may not look it to you, but I am ill. My sickness hides inside me, but eats away at my core. I may not live many more years and I don't want my skill to die with me."

"You have my sympathy, certainly, but still…why pick me?"

"You have a reputation. Your skill is unmatched, as is your work ethic. And I know your story. You are highly motivated to pursue my skill."

"Because of Rona?"

"Exactly!"

Millegran's head dropped and he stared at the ground for a long time. When he looked up, his eyes held sadness. "Anything else?"

"Yes, there is…something else." Rizzo spoke cautiously and his eyes never left the younger man's face. "I knew your father."

"My f…my father? You knew Gregan?" Few things could shake Millegran out of his melancholy, but Rizzo's words startled him.

"Yes, he was my mentor once. He was a blacksmith too, you know."

"I never met the man. Why should he care how or where I live?"

"Your father had many regrets. He wished till the end that he could make amends for his mistakes."

"Betrayal. He left my mother in poverty. It was a betrayal, not a mistake."

"Yes, he realized that. But of course, it was too late then."

"So he is dead?" It surprised Millegran that he felt a clump in his throat, when he spoke.

"An accident. A madman ran him down with his carriage."

"Did he run out on the man's daughter?"

Rizzo said nothing. He understood the half dwarf's misgivings. It could not have been easy without a father all those years.

They traveled a week cross-country. To Millegran, who had never ventured beyond the valley, which sheltered his small village, it seemed like a journey of marvels. For a time, he even forgot his ever present sadness and looked fresh-faced and curious at the colorful terrain. The rigid, sharp peeks of the mountains gave way to soft rolling hills and meadows strewn with wildflowers. Where once he had known only creeks, mere threads of icy water, sprung from the mouths of giant glaciers, he now bathed his feet in tepid rivers and lakes, where waterfowl made their nests and giant mud fish nibbled on his toes. They slept under open sky, wrapped in blankets. They hunted small game and cooked sweet potatoes and onions in the coals of their camp fire. Millegran took to the savage life like a duck to water.

It was a good two days before he began to miss his liquor. They had spent the evening building camp, cooking and swimming in a man-made lake and sat in silent companionship by the fire, when Millegran noticed that his hands trembled.

"If I don't get some Brandy in me soon, I'll go mad!"

Rizzo looked at him sideways. "You drink every day, friend?"

"It's the only way I sleep."

"You need a steady hand for the work I do," Rizzo warned. "Maybe you should lay off the sauce for a while."

"I've been off the sauce for a couple days now. You call this steady?" Millegran held his hands out over the fire. They shook like those of an old man.

Rizzo sighed. He pulled a pipe from his pack and began to stuff it. "This will get your mind off your troubles."

"Tobacco? How will that help me?"

Rizzo grinned. "This is no tobacco. It's from the hemp plant, like the one we use to make rope, but more potent."

He lit the pipe and took a deep drag. He held in the smoke for a long moment, before blowing out slowly. The smoke smelled acrid and strong. Millegran wrinkled his nose.

"It stinks!"

Rizzo laughed. "You'll get used to it." He passed the pipe. "Drag it down deep."

At first, Millegran thought he would choke but after a few puffs, he began to feel a calm detachment. At the same time, he experienced a slow rise of clarity, like an awareness and knowing, of things that before had puzzled him.

"I think perhaps I can sleep now," he said, after a while.

He woke up with hunger churning wild in his belly. He rummaged through his pack and found nothing edible, then dug out of the ashes the peels of last night's sweet potatoes and ate them. Darkness had not lifted yet and he had to use a torch to find his way to the lake. He stripped down and waded into the cool water. When he stood waist-deep, he thought, he could just walk out until the lake covered him and draw the water in as deeply as he had drawn the smoke, waiting for his lungs to scream and then to still forever.

Yet, he realized then that he did not wish it. For the first time since Rona left, he did not want to die. He had thought of it only from habit, but without the deep desperation which had painted so many thousand deaths in his mind over the past couple of years. Suddenly, he saw death as a possibility, but not a necessity; an option, but one he need not choose.

Not today, he thought. And not tomorrow or next week when I will learn to capture human hearts.

Millegran grew to appreciate Rizzo's pipe. They shared smoke nightly, like old friends and Millegran's hands ceased to tremble. The brooding blacksmith brightened and the furrows in his forehead disappeared. Once, when Rizzo teasingly called him a Halfling, he broke into coarse laughter, something he had forgotten how to do. And in the mirth of the moment, the quiet man found his tongue.

"So tell me, friend, more about this business of heartsmithing."

Rizzo smiled. "You'll see. I'll teach you to forge the cage just right, fine filigreed work, expertly crafted from top quality heart metal. You'll learn how to hide the clasp, so no one but you can ever open it. And I'll show you how to make the incision and place the cage, so it wraps tightly around the heart without squeezing."

"It sounds fantastic, but somehow, I believe you."

Rizzo nodded. "It is because you want to believe me that you do."

"Does it work every time?"

"So far it has. I've placed at least a hundred and your father twice as many and none of them failed."

"How did you learn of the heart metal? And how is it no one else uses it?"

"It's a special alloy your father discovered by chance. He forged it himself. No one but he and I ever learned how to make it. And now you will."

"And what if I sell or give away the secret?"

"You won't. Not once you've made your fist cage."

"How do you know my father didn't tell anyone else? With his lifestyle, he's liable to have fathered several children."

Rizzo shook his head. "None of them are blacksmiths."

"So he did have others! I have siblings somewhere."

"Don't fret about it, Millegran. They don't know about you either."

Millegran scowled. "Of course not! What man would brag about having fathered a half dwarf?"

Rizzo laid a soothing hand on Millegran's arm. "You're a blacksmith. That's something special," he said gently. "And he bragged plenty to me about that."

Surprised, Millegran leaned forward toward the fire. "He knew?"

"Who do you think paid for your apprenticeship?"

"I thought, my mother…but then, she couldn't have afforded it, could she?"

Rizzo didn't answer. Sometimes it was better for a man to figure things out for himself.

They arrived in the city after ten days' travel. What a marvel for Millegran who had never seen buildings so tall or alleys so narrow! After a few steps on the cobblestones, he donned his heavy wooden shoes, uncaring that people turned to look when they heard his foot falls. Never one to give much mind to what others thought, he assumed an air of stolid defiance after Rona left.

If they chose to stare, Millegran stared back openly. So many humans in one place! And they dressed in such finery. Even the men, who rushed from home to work place, wore trousers, shirts and coats of such quality that Millegran almost wanted to touch them. Rizzo's clothing seemed coarse in comparison, his own resembled tree trunks. The women, however, promenaded in glossy silks and satins and smooth velvets. Never in his life had Millegran dreamed of anything so beautiful.

When they turned down a shaded back alley, he could smell the smithy. The forge called him in, like a beacon to his new home. He quickened his step and so did Rizzo. The heartsmith unlocked the heavy oak door and waved Millegran in. Out of habit, Millegran stooped at the door, but realized, he did not have to and walked through upright, head held high.

It looked like gold, the heart metal, laid out on the table by the forge and it gleamed against the smoke-stained interior of the smithy.

"This is it?" asked Millegran and the heartsmith nodded. "It looks too delicate to have any strength."

"That's deceptive. It is harder than iron and must be forged under high heat. It breaks my tools if I'm not careful."

"Can't you make the tools out of this?"

Rizzo shook his head. "It is too precious to waste."

The following weeks were a revelation to the half dwarf. Although he spent many hours in the forge, learning to work the heart metal, he also met Rizzo's clients, desperate men and women, who turned to the heartsmith after all else had failed.

"My wife…she seems so different now. Ever since…well, I think she has another lover. I haven't caught her yet. I don't want to. If I prove right my suspicions, I'll have to do something about it. Much rather, I would like to turn her back to me, without knowing the truth."

"This man wants to marry me, but I must be sure that I will always be his only love."

"My son has obsessed over this girl for years now, but is too shy to ask her out. If she marries another man, he will die of loneliness. I must find a way for her to notice him."

"My mother has grieved so since my father's death. There is a man, who secretly loves her, but she sees in him only a friend. He could make her happy again, if only she gave him a chance. Can you help her?"

Millegran listened – and learned. And he, who for so long had only seen his own sadness, saw how many others were also suffering, weeping, and giving up on life. In his eyes, Rizzo became a hero, one who gave to the lonely their heart's desire.

The more Millegran learned, the more compassionate he became, and the greater grew his own sense of power. Yet, it wasn't until he assisted Rizzo in placing a cage that he understood the scope of his reach.

When he wasn't working or listening to Rizzo, Millegran explored the city. He had traded his wooden shoes for a pair of Rizzo's leather boots and people seemed less apt to stare. The streets of the city ran North-South and East-West. From them, short alleys branched off to divide the rows of houses. Most businesses lined the main streets, while residences huddled in back alleys. One day, from one of those back alleys emerged a figure that made Millegran's heart want to stop.

She was still as lovely, although less cheerful than he remembered. Her face showed a mature, settled quality and her gait seemed not as lively. She strode confidently, but with her eyes on the cobblestone pavement and so did not see him. He had it in his throat to call her name, but then resisted. As much as he craved her, he feared her as well. She had rejected him once. She might well do it again.

He committed the alley to memory and returned to the smithy, where Rizzo stood, bent over a piece of heart metal.

"Rizzo, I need a cage!" His voice rose and fell with emotion.

The heartsmith laid down his tools and rose to full height. "You saw Rona!"

"Did you know she lived here in the city?" There was pain in Millegran's face and something else. Did the one man whom he trusted, betray him also?

Yet, Rizzo shook his head. "No, but I thought it possible."

"You should have warned me."

"And got your hopes up? I think not. I would not be so cruel."

Millegran seemed to droop. His hands hung by his sides and his eyes clouded. "I have to have her. I still miss her so much."

"It may not be so easy. You know nothing of her life here."

"Please, friend. If you care anything about me!"

Rizzo sighed. "Very well. But I must warn you: There are consequences when you capture a heart. And if you change your mind, know that it is much harder to remove a cage than to place one. Freedom always comes with a price."

While Rizzo crafted the cage, Millegran lurked about Rona's back alley until he saw her through a window move about her house. He marked her door with a chalk and returned to the smithy. "I'm ready when you are."

Rizzo handed him a heart cage. It was especially fine. Rizzo had fashioned it with all his skill and all his compassion.

"You've watched me enough times and you've done some practice incisions. Now it is your turn to cut. Do you want my assistance?"

Millegran shook his head. "I know what to do."

He arrived at Rona's home after dark. For a blacksmith, it is easy to open a locked door and he entered silently. Barefoot, he sneaked through the house and found her sleeping beside a young man, a human.

For safety, he drugged them both with chloroform. For a moment, he stood, watching her, then freed her lovely chest and placed the knife. On the side, above her left breast, he cut, sliding the knife at an angle. If he cut too deep, he could sever an artery, too shallow, and the cage would not slip in.

He found that he held his breath. His whole life seemed reduced to this one moment, when he would capture forever the heart of the woman he loved.

The placement went well. The cage slipped in easily and traveled to wrap gently around Rona's heart. He gathered her into his arms and carried her from the bed chamber and out through the door into the alley. She would sleep for a while yet. She weighed light in his arms, as light as his heart felt, now that he once again feasted his eyes on her.

He carried her into the smithy and to the bed in the back room. There he lay with her until she woke, cradling her in his strong arms. Rizzo stepped out the front door to give them privacy.

Rona's eyes clouded with confusion when she awakened. Yet, while the drug still caged her mind, her heart surged for the young smith, who waited, breathlessly, for her first words.

"My love," she said. "Why did you take so long to find me?"

His bliss reigned all week. Rizzo worked alone in the smithy, while Millegran and Rona walked along the river in sunshine, kissed under the stars and heated the bed with their love. Then, one day, Rizzo admitted a man to the smithy, who held by the hand a small child. The man's eyes darkened with sadness, when he saw Millegran and Rona emerge from the bed chamber, hair towseled and skin glistening with spent heat.

"I should kill you," he said to the half dwarf, "but I fear that would bring me nothing. She would only die a weeping widow and leave me and the child to grieve her passing."

Millegran looked to the heartsmith, who nodded. "These are Rona's mate and child. When you caged her heart, she forgot that she loved them. Now the child is without a mother, and you have broken this man's heart."

"She was mine first. He stepped onto another man's territory."

Rizzo sighed. "You do not own a lover."

"Say you who taught me how to capture one!"

"One should only capture a free heart. Rona's was not free."

"She was mine before."

"And she left you years ago to make another life for herself. Can you truly build happiness on this man's pain? Can you buy joy with this child's abandonment?"

"Leave me!" roared the half dwarf, picked up a hammer and brandished it. "I cannot breathe with you crowding my space."

They all left, except Rona, who's eyes searched Millegran's face without understanding.

"We can take the child, if you wish it," said Millegran.

Rona furrowed her forehead. "What child?"

At last, Millegran grasped the depth of his transgression. He embraced the woman, who had occupied his every thought for so long and carried her back into the bed chamber. He kissed her and when her eyes were closed, drugged her once more with chloroform. Her incision had barely healed. He cut easily through the tender flesh. With a long hook, he undid the clasp and loosened the cage. It gave some resistance, but after only a week, it still released easily and slipped out through the incision into Millegran's hand. There was more blood this time, and he worked quickly to seal the wound.

While she was still sleeping, he kissed her once more. She would no longer love him when she woke.

He tore away from her, his heart broken a second time. And this time, he did not find the strength to resist the call of death. He took the knife, still bloodied, and plunged it deep into his own heart. He fell on top of Rona and wept, while his life blood spilled from his chest wound. When Rizzo returned to find him, his heart beat had faded until it ceased and the young smith was no more.

"Oh, if only I had told him the truth!" cried the man, who called himself Rizzo, but who was once known as Gregan. Twice, he had made the journey to the distant valley, once as a young buck, eager for love and adventure, a second time to find Millegran and make amends. The cages he had built were weak, beside the web that strangled his own heart, and he now came to collect the wages of his old sins. And in the twilight of the smithy, Gregan fell to his knees and wept, spilling years of regret over the body of his dead son.

The Portal

Every afternoon at three, Mietz, the cat, vanished from sight. One minute she could be seen sitting at the edge of the wood as though in deep contemplation, the next minute, Mietz was gone. But, when night fell, and Hillary called frantically from the kitchen door, Mietz came bounding up the driveway and leapt into Hillary's open arms. She trembled, and her little heart raced, and she rubbed against her worried guardian's face, kneaded her shoulder with busy paws, stuck her nose in Hillary's ear and purred loudly.

Every day it was the same: sudden disappearance, excited return. Hillary tried to find her in those afternoons, walked through the woods, calling, rattling a box of kitty treats, but to no avail. Between three o'clock in the afternoon and darkness, Mietz did not exist.

Mietz discovered the portal by accident. She had slipped past it at first, chasing a dragonfly, which she had knocked out of the air twice before it escaped her. Mietz groomed furiously for a minute to soothe her temper and then settled in the shade, tucking her front paws under. It was a warm afternoon, although autumn had turned greens into golds and reds, and the leaves were falling. Mietz dozed for a while. She didn't feel hungry; she was well fed. The dragonfly was intended for dessert and for entertainment only. Her tufted ears twitched away a pesky fly, and she rolled onto her side to stretch. She squeezed her eyes shut against the ray of light which poked through the tree branches and so didn't notice it right away. It wasn't until the pads on her left forepaw felt cold and wet that she opened her eyes and realized, *her paw was missing!*

She leaped back and found her paw attached to her foreleg as it should be, but when she sniffed it, a wintery scent emerged from it. She licked the warmth back into it and puzzled. Then, cautiously, eyes large and wide with fear, back arched and fur spiked high, she advanced toward the spot where she had been resting. She prodded. She poked. Her paw disappeared in nothingness. She remained rigid for a moment, feeling the sensation of chilled sogginess, but then curiosity won, and she stepped into the portal and emerged at the foot of a snow-covered mountain, shaking slush from her paws.

Mietz crouched. Her new surroundings invited no ease of vigilance. Ears folded back, eyes wide and black from widened pupils, she waited, every muscle tensed to leap back to safety. Yet, no monsters emerged, no dogs, no cars, and after a while, Mietz relaxed and began to explore her new surroundings.

For the most part, they were wet. While snow lay thick on the mountain slopes, in the valley where Mietz padded, it had melted, and she bounded to a higher and drier spot shaking all four feet. She reached a boulder and hauled herself up the side of it with back legs scrabbling at wet stone.

The view from the boulder stunned her to stillness. Before her, a valley of rocks and snow stretched to the far reaches of her vision. Long and narrow, carved by a river, it wound between craggy peaks which loomed above the boulder upon which she crouched. While the snow had melted to slush by the portal, farther downstream, winter seemed to have a good hold on the ground, and snow sparkled faintly in dim light. A breath of almost warmth hovered at the entry point but faded to frost just a few feet inward. While she watched, the air grew colder, and slush turned to ice, closing the little cat into a world of deep winter.

Mietz shivered. Her coat had shed its winter hair long ago. She had just finished summer in her world, and autumn had not yet bitten her enough to grow more. She spiked her thin fur out to retain as much warmth as possible and purred to soothe herself. After a while, she grew hungry; the chilled air elevated her metabolism, and her morning meal now seemed hours ago. She leapt off the boulder and trekked through the snow down to the river, hoping to find some sign of life. The frozen snow carried her easily but her journey ended in disappointment when she found no fish in the frigid water and no lizards or frogs or even crickets at its edge. Mietz did what any house-cat might do when she finds herself in a precarious situation. She meowed. First quietly, timidly, then louder, yowling out her hunger, her fear and her loneliness.

A sudden sound silenced her. Ears perked and whiskers aquiver, she listened. She opened her mouth and scented. Unmoving, like a statue, she remained at river's edge while a shadowy form bounded across the snow toward her. Paws padded lightly, fur brushed ground and Mietz caught the scent of a creature she had never before seen or smelled.

A few paces in front of Mietz, the creature halted. Any other time, Mietz would have run for cover, but something held her there, staring large-eyed at the strange, furry creature which towered over her perhaps twice as tall as any human. A thought formed in the little cat's mind. Not really like words, cats don't do that. But it was still a question, and she posed it to the creature in thought and gesture.

"Who are you?"

The creature equally did not speak and Mietz would not have expected it to. But its scent grew stronger, it shifted its feet, six of them, and by smell and movement gave an almost imperceptible answer.

"I am the Supreme Being of this world."

The little tabby crouched. She had never met a Supreme Being and wasn't sure if she should run and hide or stay and fight. Another question formed in her head.

"Why am I here?"

The Supreme Being shifted and rustled, and the answer came to the little cat without words.

"Because you were curious."

"Is this a bad thing?"

"No it is not. I wished for you to come."

The little cat sat a little straighter. Her ears twitched, and she blinked.

"Why?"

"Because you must bring your human."

For a long while, the cat and the Supreme Being spoke. Not in words, of course. Cats can't do that. Perhaps six-legged, furry Supreme Beings do not either. The conversation consisted of movement and scent, mostly, with an occasional grunt from the Supreme Being and might have translated into something like this:

"Long ago, this world lay bathed in sunshine. There was no frost unless I wished it. The river flowed wide as this valley every spring, and the land grew fertile under the cover of water. Then, the river receded into its bed, and summer glowed over the peaks. The river and its banks teemed with life and so did the valley and the mountain slopes. The meadows abounded with flowers in colors so rich, they made my soul ache. All this was mine alone, and I reveled in it."

"What happened to this world, Supreme Being?"

"Not so fast, little one. I'll come to that. When summer had reached its peak, the winds began to turn, and cooler air flattered the trees until their leaves began to blush. This was called Autumn."

"I know Autumn. It reigns in my world now. I chase the leaves when they fall"

"I had all this, and all life was subject to me. I hunted and killed only what I needed. The creatures of this world revered me yet showed no fear when, once sated, I walked among them. How could any Supreme Being be more blessed than I was?"

"I can't imagine this world with flowers and animals."

"Close your eyes and I'll show you."

The little cat obeyed, and in her mind, images began to form. She saw meadows with rich golden grasses and flowers in warm reds and purples, trees of deepest green, branches trailing to the ground from the weight of sweet fruit. The river ran clear or blue at its greatest depths. Silver shimmered the fish which flitted through the water in abundant schools. Frogs and lizards clung to roots and leaves at water's edge, and the grass quivered from many little rodents running through it. Larger rodents and hoofed animals grazed the hillsides, and Supreme Being moved among them with pelt and eyes shining.

"Why did it change, Supreme Being?"

"My fault." The creature began to droop. All six feet shifted, and its eyes closed tightly.

"I became too full of myself. I desired greater things and more, craved worlds outside this one, wanted beings more like myself to dominate. I devised a way to enter the human world. Only once, I did that, but it was enough to condemn this world as well as theirs. The river itself rose to curse me and curse this valley where I remain, waiting for someone to break the spell and return this world to its former beauty."

"What happened to the humans?"

"I brought them desire. I infected them with longing and craving and the need to dominate. I brought badness into your world, little one. Humans call me the Devil."

"I do not know about human ways. I am a cat."

"Indeed you are. And that is why I need you. You must bring your human."

"Why?"

"Because only a human can break the spell."

"But why my human? Why not another?"

"Your human has shown unselfish love for you, a furred creature. That is what I need."

"Why can't the human find the Portal?"

"Because she has lost curiosity. She knows, so she no longer has a need to wonder."

"Tell me what to do," said the little cat, her small back straight, and her eyes bright.

"Take this seed and plant it at the entrance to the portal. It will not grow here, but your world has warmth. In Spring, when the seed has sprouted, lead your human to the plant."

"Just that?"

"Yes, just that."

"Can I come visit you again?"

"Any time you like, but the portal only opens for a while each day."

When Mietz rushed into Hillary's arms that night, her heart was full of the things she had seen and heard. She rubbed her face against Hillary's cheek and purred loudly, but Hillary didn't understand what so excited the little tabby. She petted and hugged and kissed her, crying out, "I was so worried about you!"

Every day after that, Mietz slipped through the portal, and every night, she greeted Hillary with the same enthusiasm. She planted the seed, as she had been told, and when Spring came, a plant grew there like no plant anywhere in the human world. The leaves stood squared, like a four leaf clover, but succulent with silver veins and a thick, furred stem. Mietz couldn't resist rubbing against the plant, but it didn't break, its leaves yielded to pressure and sprang back as soon as she moved away.

Mietz began to call out to Hillary, giving her most pitiful mews, so she would run from the house worried. Mietz faked a limp and meowed in the most heartbreaking tones until Hillary followed. At the portal, the tabby stopped and dropped to the ground next to the strange plant. Hillary, in her worry, did not notice right away, but picked Mietz up and carried her inside to check her over. Mietz recovered instantly and demanded to be let outside with fierce yowling. Hillary complied and followed.

For several days, this circus continued, until Hillary at last noticed the silver-leafed plant. She bent over it and touched it with gentle fingers. When she did, her heart opened, and wonder returned, and she looked around with wide eyes.

"What a wonderful plant," she murmured. "Mietz, did you see that? I've never seen anything like it."

Mietz purred, pushed ahead into the portal and vanished. Hillary cried out. And took a step. And the portal opened wide and let her through into the world of ice and snow.

Mietz, familiar with the valley, bounded toward the river, and the human followed. Wherever Hillary stepped snow melted, and grass began to sprout. When she bent to take a drink from the river, the ice receded, and the banks greened, giving life to the stark landscape.

Mietz had run ahead, looking for Supreme Being, and Hillary shouted after her. The wind picked up her voice and carried it across the hillsides and up to the dark peaks. Everywhere it reached, snow vanished, and life returned.

From holes in the ground, insects emerged, then reptiles and eventually rodents. Birds swooshed through the air on splendid wings. A vivid sun rose over the peaks and bathed the valley in golden light. Small fair weather clouds formed overhead.

Finally, Supreme Being loped down from the heights, fur gleaming and flowing in the breeze. It bowed to the human, and Hillary, awed by its unfamiliar appearance, bowed in return.

Supreme Being did not speak, but its bearing and the brightness of its eyes relayed the message which echoed in Hillary's mind.

"Thank you, human. You have restored my world. You and the cat are forever welcome here."

Hillary inclined her head, not knowing what to say to this speechless creature. She picked up Mietz who snaked herself around Hillary's neck. She moved toward the portal, then turned around for a last look.

Supreme Being glowed with joy, surrounded by animals in a field of purple flowers. Never again would it allow ambition to take hold. Never again would it give in to unreasonable desire. With the human and the cat as welcome and frequent visitors, its world was complete.

Hillary smiled. She felt younger yet at once wiser, too. Never again would she allow worry to obscure her sense of wonder. She vowed to return often and walk in this golden world, where six-legged creatures spoke without speaking. Her heart skipped with joy, and she squeezed her little cat gently.

And Mietz? Mietz, the cat seemed most satisfied of all.

Crystal Demon

He rides the ocean waves at night fall, concealed by twilight. You'll hear him, but first, there is no true sound, only a precognition, which makes your skin crawl, and fine hairs stand up on your body. After a few minutes, you'll hear a 'swish!' or a 'whoosh' with tiny, tinkling overtones, like miniature glass wind chimes. You don't want to be in the water then.

Natives think, he was born in Galveston Bay and still lives there, but he avoids the city. Maybe the lights confuse him, or perhaps he doesn't like the seawall. But when he gets hungry, usually on a moonless night, he seeks out Crystal Beach, where the unsuspecting camp and play by the water after dark.

I was one of those late night adventurers, and I escaped him by sheer luck. Dorian, my lover, was not so fortunate. May he rest in peace.

You may think of this demon as some sort of sea monster, but you are mistaken. His nature is not so crude. He does not pull you down with brute force. Nor does he stomp out on the sand and leave foot prints. He is not that tangible.

He hides in foam crests and peeks over tall breakers. When he is near, the smell of salt intensifies. Fish flee him, and frustrated fishermen pack up their gear and leave. The ocean seems dead, but for him who haunts it.

Campers in the know zip up their tents and huddle with the lamps on. But if they had too much to drink, they may not feel it in time. Dorian and I were drinking heavily that night. We were in the middle of a fight and we both made the most of it by clutching our brandy flasks and sulking. I called him 'Dor' most of the time, but when I was angry, it became 'Dork.' I still regret flinging that name at him on that particular night.

No one is quite sure how the demon feeds, but we know, his victims' brains turn to mush and their insides curdle. He doesn't venture far from the water and Dor would have been quite safe, had he stayed at the camp site.

I had called him 'Dork' one too many times, and he rose abruptly, flung his flask on the sand and sauntered off toward the water.

The sky darkened. I don't know how else to describe it. It was night, but somehow, it became more *nightly*. The thunder of the ocean crescendoed, wind whooshed, and I heard fine glass chime. The scent in the air thickened. It was a warm scent but fat and full. The sudden absence of all fishy odors gave it a dead quality, and it swelled to a sickening stench.

"Dor," I cried out. "Watch out!" But, his feet already flopped across soft mud, and teaser waves licked at his toes. "Something's not right, Dor!"

He staggered. The brandy had taken its toll. He had no business being in the water. The wind whipped his shoulder-long hair into the air, making him look like a frazzled scare crow. I noticed how thin he was. I envied him his fast metabolism, but now his slender silhouette looked gaunt against the wide horizon. Fear for his safety smashed into my chest and choked me. What if I lost him?

Dorian waded into the churning sea. I might have gone after him then and saved him, but I sat, spellbound by my own fierce emotions. I did not love him any less than I did in our first glorious year. Why did we argue so much?

And then, Dorian cried out. His voice rose to best the ocean's thunder He keened with a tremendous, overpowering madness. He threw his head back and screamed to the sinister sky, and his body rocked and swayed.

With a shout, I leapt to my feet and raced to aid him. Sand scattered and flew, and the thick air tortured my lungs. I fell over a piece of drift wood and scrambled on hands and knees to reach him. The chimes intensified to a deafening clank. The wind howled as if through a maze of glass tubes. And still, Dorian keened.

I think he saw me. He turned toward me for a moment, but then, he spun away and waded into the rising surf. For a moment, I felt something brush my cheek, and I felt as though someone had split my head open with an axe. Then the demon was gone, and I clutched the wet sand and wept. I struggled to my knees and stared at the horizon, where Dorian plunged screaming into the sea to perish.

For a few minutes, the winds continued to rage, the chimes continued to ring, and the darkness continued to hover. I sat, unbelieving on my haunches and stared at the churning sea. But then, almost suddenly, the storm settled. The blackness lifted, and stars blinked on a cloudless sky. The air sweetened. I sucked giant gulps of it into my hungry lungs.

On the muddy shore lay Dorian's battered body. I crawled to hold him, to clutch his head to my chest and cover his face with kisses. Eyes still wide and mouth rigid in a frozen scream, he looked like a stranger. For a long time, I wept and cursed the Crystal demon who had taken him.

I packed our belongings the next morning. I said my goodbyes to Dorian who lay in a simple coffin at the local funeral home. I had arranged for his body to be shipped back to Waco where his mother lived. When I drove away from the coast, zipping in and out of traffic, I swore, never to return to Crystal Beach or anywhere near Galveston Bay. To this day, I have kept that promise.

Nightingale

If you think the small, insignificant bird which landed on your window and tweeted so sweetly triggered your homesick longing, you weren't paying close enough attention.

It is an easy mistake to make. Although the modest brown Passerine astonishes with its warbles, trills and gurgles, it does not wrench your heart. What soars beyond it is the true source of your pain and is the sole reason for the small bird's nightly call.

If you could understand the songster's language, you might hasten to close your window, pull the covers over your head and pray. If you could heed his warning, you might save yourself from slicing your wrists with shards of broken glass and watching your life pulse away onto the stone floor.

You call him Nightingale, yet the one who bears that name lurks in the shadows and rides the autumn winds. The bird is only its herald. You will listen to his lovely call at your peril. Danger follows behind him. Do not linger at the window if you mean to live into the next year.

Nightingale swoops not from the sky but rises from the depths of Yffern. Its wings are not of flesh and blood but spun from darkest despair. You will not see it against the night sky, yet its many-colored shimmering coat confounds and taunts the eye like a three-dimensional illusion.

Its name hints at its true nature and was given by distraught sailors eons ago. Storm-battered prayers rising from trembling lips begged mercy. "Do not let us perish in this tempest. Do not let night fall on us in this gale!"

And yet, night fell, and men drowned while Nightingale sucked life from their souls and blood from their bodies. Did they hear the bird sing, just before the horrid creature struck? Perhaps they did, but we shall never know.

Last night, the warbler sang behind my home. I ran to close my windows, lock my doors, and light my white candles against the dread that would surely follow. My gratitude to the small bird for his warning! I am still alive today.

Outside my door, my true love lies sprawling, his eyes broken. His hand clutches a letter still, yet his wrists are sliced, and the blood has long since stopped flowing. Did he ring my doorbell? Did he try to speak to me? I cry out, and with trembling fingers dial the paramedics, although I know that his life is already spent.

In the morning sun, a tiny brown bird raises his wings. He does not sing today.

Song Of The Ocean

Ayafari was not a goddess or queen or heroine of any kind, and she never became famous. She died as humbly as she lived, in a hut built from driftwood and dried seaweed. No one remembers her name now, yet they should, and they should acknowledge her importance because she was the one who wrote the song the ocean sings.

The girl with the strange name was born a fisherman's daughter. Her cradle was made of a hollowed log, the kind fishermen used to glide through water, but smaller. It had been carved and burned and carved some more by generations of fishermen sitting beside their huts with hands never idle and hearts filled with joy over the approaching birth of their first child. It had been lined with cushions and linens lovingly stitched from sack cloth and pieces of old clothing by young mothers and gray-haired grandmothers. Into this heirloom she was laid, after being washed in the sacred waters of the sea, and she balled her little fists and wailed. Her mother placed one foot on the cradle and gently rocked, rocked, rocked her, and finally, the child quieted and opened her sea-blue eyes.

In those days, the ocean didn't have a song, and seaside dwellers did not love the sea but feared him. In those days, fishermen wished for strong sons to carry on their work, and Ayafari's father, after looking at his daughter and learning she was the wrong sex, turned away and did not speak another word to her or to his wife who gave birth to her.

Ayafari grew up without the sound of a man's voice. Only her mother's gentle words crooned her to sleep. And so, when the child began to speak, her first word was 'mother' and her second word, 'sea.' And the man who came and went in silence and brought fresh catch from his boat to the table became 'the fish-man.'

The year Ayafari learned to walk, her mother miscarried an infant boy and, the year after, another, and the fisherman, giving up all hope of having a son, beat his grieving wife to death in a drunken rage. He might have killed his young daughter as well, had she not scrambled to a neighbor's hut for shelter.

Life by the sea is not gentle. Ayafari did not return home to her murderous father, but neither did she find a loving family among those who dwelt near the harbor. The fisher folk fed her scraps when she came begging, and from time to time someone took pity and gave her an old piece of clothing or a blanket or took her inside to give her a proper bath, but for the most part, she slept under open sky and ate garbage. She combed her hair with fingers and tied it back with fishing line. She bit her nails, yes, even her toe nails. Her feet, unencumbered by shoes, grew broad and hard.

Despite all the hardship, Ayafari grew into a strong, healthy young woman. She was not ugly but she was a wild thing, tanned to dark leather and hair streaming in tangles to her hips. Sometimes, a light came into her eyes that frightened the fisher folk, and none of the young men wanted anything to do with her. By the time she was old enough to have been wed, the sea had become her only lover.

And the sea did love her. When she walked along the shore barefoot, waves spilled around her feet ever so gently, and the sand grew rich with rare and beautiful shells. Gulls alit on her shoulders and dropped fish into waiting hands. She never went hungry again. She gathered seashells and sold them to a vendor at the tourist market. She built a hut from drift wood and seaweed, and she sat on a cliff and sang. She never learned to read but she didn't need to; the sea provided everything.

She sang to the ocean, her lover, a special song, sitting alone on a rock, salt spray in her face. No one but the sea listened; no one but the sea cared. The fisher folks sat in their huts at night, mending their nets and rocking their babies, and the young men and women danced and played pool and went skinny dipping after dark. Ayafari, who had no concept of happiness, felt free.

One night, a group of tourists strolled through town, looking for trouble. Bored with the pool hall and the sappy music, they headed out to the cliffs with jugs of whiskey and bottles of pills in their hands. They stumbled over rocks and slipped on wet ground but they didn't let it deter them. Gradually, they made it out to Ayafari's cliff dwelling. They plundered the hut, finding nothing of value, except some shells and a few blankets, woven from seaweed. Suddenly, a song floated toward them on the wind, a melody of such eerie beauty, it raised goose bumps on their skin. They followed the sound to the edge of the cliff and found Ayafari, wild of hair and eye. They pulled her from the cliff and dragged her back to the hut. Ayafari screamed, and the sea who heard her began to churn.

How long does it take to gang rape a young woman? How much does she suffer? How long to beat her and rip fistfuls of wild, glorious hair from her head? They didn't waste much time, and when she fought too hard, they hit her over the head with a whiskey bottle. She never got back up.

Outside, the sea clawed and worried at the cliff face. He smelled blood and violence and raged after the rapists who staggered back toward the city. But it takes time for an ocean to build up to full fury; it was almost daybreak before a tidal wave washed over the city without warning, drowning all who slept there.

They all died, evildoers, fishermen, children, the sea made no distinction. His revenge was so terrible that no house was left standing, no boat left docked at the harbor. The bodies washed out to sea and were never found, except Ayafari's. Her cliff stayed dry, and her hut, where she lay lifeless and pale, head crusted with dried blood, only swayed gently in the wind.

The sea can never forget her, and he sings her song still, the song of waves and water, fish and salt, wind and love. And by that song, Ayafari lives on.

To Stop A Burning

Thalia braced against the wind, which tore at her billowing black dress and alternated between pushing her embroidered velvet jacket tight against her body and pulling it open to expose her slender neck and the pentagram which dangled on a golden chain between her breasts. She gripped an equally embroidered bag of sacred herbs, as though the wind spirits might rip it from her hands and carry it to the distant woods.

"Call them again, Ray," she said softly to her companion, a young man, whose dark hair hung in a tight braid down his back, and who struggled to hold down his tall, pointed black hat. His long, satiny black coat, buttoned to the neck and covered in sequins resembled a sparkling firmament. His free hand wielded what at first glance appeared to be an umbrella with a handle so intricately carved into the image of a cat, it seemed alive and ready to spring. A second look revealed that it was a thing of mystery, wand-like and slender, with black ribbons flowing around the hilt.

"They're coming," he said, just as quietly. "I can feel them."

They huddled in the shadows of an ancient mansion, which shielded them from a blood-red setting sun. A light shone from upstairs, where in Reverend Mother's office a shadowy figure ghosted from window to window.

With a sudden 'whoosh,' a cloud of dust rose, and two brooms alit next to them on the sidewalk. As one, they reached for them, she choosing the larger, sturdier one, and he as the gentleman giving way.

"Ride like the wind," she called over her shoulder as they mounted. "We have no time to waste!"

In darkness, behind thick dungeon walls, three women huddled. Wrists and ankles bled from heavy irons which enclosed them. Clothes hung in tatters from gaunt bodies, long hair fell in tangles past bony shoulders.

On first glance, these three seemed like sisters, but how they endured, how they were able to bear the horrors around them showed their differences. While two prayed fervently for the Lord to convince the Church of their innocence, for they had done nothing unseemly, the third woman remained silent. Her eyes, though worn and tired from suffering, showed none of the urgent despair so commonly seen in Inquisition chambers. Of all the women who had passed through these walls and found their death at the hands of the priests, this one would be the only true witch.

Her cell mates, while drawing comfort from her presence, still eyed her with suspicion. In the weeks since their capture, this woman had not wept, nor prayed, nor begged for mercy. The burn marks on her arms and legs had healed faster than theirs, and her broken bones had mended. While her screams rang just as loudly across the court yard during the questionings, and her blood ran just as red, they suspected she was not like them.

"Why do you not pray with us, Marissa," the younger one asked. "Do you not have faith in the Lord our Savior?"

Which Lord? Which savior? The one who lets his church burn women by the hundreds from mere fear of them?

She did not say it aloud. Their plight tugged at her heart more even than her own. She wanted to throw her arms around them and take away their pain, but if she had, they would know her for what she was. She would not have blamed them if they had chosen to betray her to the inquisitors and reduce their own suffering.

She sighed and produced a small rosary. Her lips prayed familiar prayers, but her soul did not participate in the ritual of the men priests who held her captive.

Outside the walls, a raven called. Marissa did not flinch but her heart skipped a beat when she recognized the voice of her familiar.

"Look, we've been spotted." Raynier pointed to the horizon, where furtive shadows scurried across the last gleam of crimson light. "They've let the falcons loose."

Thalia spurred her broom, and it lurched, speeding her ahead of her companion. He tapped the neck of his broom and closed the gap quickly. "Don't worry; they are still a good distance away."

Thalia's taut smile betrayed her tension. Flying into a cast of falcons could down any witch. They would have to out-fly them or go in for a landing and wait until dark to continue.

"At least they don't know what we are yet. We're up too high."

She reached across and clasped Raynier's hand, and together they sped away from the winged menace toward the distant Black Forest.

They arrived by moon light and landed safely at the edge of a large clearing. A fire beckoned in the center of a stone circle. A scent of myrrh and sandalwood greeted the travelers. Perhaps a hundred men and women sat cross-legged in the grass in groups of five or more. Others wandered between groups or worked spells by the fire. Thalia spoke a password and she and Raynier approached a stooped figure by the burn pit.

"We came as soon as we heard, Blessed Mother! Our own Reverend Mother still lingers to gather the last of the coven. She sends her love."

The stooped figure, a gray haired crone, embraced the pair warmly. "Thank you for coming so quickly. We truly have no time to waste."

"We brought some sacred herbs. We hope they will aid in our cause. We live in dark times, do we not, Blessed Mother?"

"Indeed we do, young daughter and thank you for the offering. I hope we may speed our world toward the Light." She pointed. "Your people are over there. You may want to join them."

Brother Adrian sprawled on the stone floor of his tiny cell and wept. Cold crept through his thin robe and raised chills on bony arms and legs. Large unsightly ears stood pale against his shaven head. Teeth chattered under blue lips. The only warm things about Brother Adrian were his tears. In his wretchedness, the monk felt unworthy to pray or even kneel but pressed his cheek and emaciated body to the tiles in utter capitulation.

In the beginning, he had wept for the women. Their plight had torn at his conscience, their screams cut like cold steel into his heart, and guilt had nearly suffocated him. But, more recently, he cried mostly for himself, for the sad state of his body, at the brink of starvation, and the sadder state of his soul. He lamented Father Benedict's anger, his own ineptness, his ever-present loneliness and fear. Wordlessly, he sprawled, in abject penance for a sin he could not remember committing.

Only scant light stole through a crack under the heavy pine door, leaving him huddled in gloom. In the corner of his cell stood a bowl of thin, gray gruel, no bread and no spoon to eat with. No pallet beckoned for him to rest his weary head, no blanket promised comfort. He had water, he had gruel, and he had an empty bucket for his waste. He had tried, at first, to keep track of his days of confinement, as the scratches in the stone wall showed, but after so many months in near night he lost count, and hope, and the need to know.

Once in a while, when he wrenched a confession from one of the broken wretches he tormented, the monks brought him up from the dungeon. Father allowed him to bathe and wash his robe. He gave him fresh bread and wine and on occasion a sliver of meat. For a day, Adrian would walk in the cloister and feel the gentle touch of a fresh breeze on his gaunt face, the warmth of a summer sun. For a day, he felt sated and the gnawing in his belly quieted. For a day, his soul sang, filled with kind words from his holy brethren.

Elena, the Reverend Mother paced in her study, wringing her hands and murmuring incantations. Her gaunt face glistened with perspiration although no fire burned in the hearth and cold shadows lurked in every corner. She felt the urgency of her mission in the pulsing of her blood and the aching of her bones. Once more she reached out to the members of her coven. She sensed them all but one. Of all her charges, only Marissa had not responded to her call, though she tried every spell she knew. Reverend Mother trembled, her heart crawling up her throat from fear. Of all the witches in all the covens, would it be her darling youngest daughter, estranged from her own coven, in the hands of the tormentors?

She cast yet another spell and waited, holding her breath to keep from missing a sound. After a while, a rush of wings reached her ears, and then, with a loud caw, a Raven alit on her window sill. She opened the window and the bird hopped inside, its head tilted to one side, its intelligent eyes watching her every move.

"Where is she? Why didn't she come with you?"

The Raven shook its feathers and let its head droop. It crouched and folded its ebony wings over its head. Imprisoned! Marissa was the one!

Two silent tears fell from Reverend Mother's eyes but she only hesitated a moment. Reaching with one hand for her sturdy old broom, she gestured toward the window with the other.

"Go back to her! Bring her comfort. We will do everything we can."

She leapt onto her broom and flew out the window. There was not a moment to lose.

Marissa woke to the caw of the raven. It was a quiet caw and did not stir her cellmates from slumber. Marissa rose silently and tiptoed to the wall, willing her chains not to clank. A gap at the top of the wall, braced with iron bars represented the only window. It was too far up for her to see out, but she could smell the night air. Her jailers had unhooked her chains from the heavy iron ball to give her a taste of freedom. Each night one of the women, and this was her night. They told her she could walk out unhindered if only she confessed. Such was always their promise. Marissa knew it to be a lie.

The raven poked his black head between the bars and eyed her thoughtfully. He was too big to squeeze in, so he crouched on the ledge and watched her. He cawed again and Marissa felt comforted. Her mother knew, and she would find a way to help!

Marissa was a talented witch but her powers didn't suffice to break her from bondage. Her gifts lie toward healing and growing things. She could make a dead stick sprout and burst into bloom but in this dungeon of stone and steel, there was nothing for her to grow. Her soul ached for the outdoors, for the scent of moss and heather, the feel of rain on bare skin, of wind to tousle her hair. She longed to once again run her hands over rough tree bark or plunge them into wet, fertile earth, to race barefoot through soft, dew-moist grass. How long had it been? She had lost count. It had to have been many moons, since she walked in sunshine.

Had Marissa still belonged to a coven, someone would have learned of her imprisonment long ago but she was a solitary witch, a fact she regretted bitterly.

If I get out alive, I will rejoin my mother's coven. How will she receive me? Can we set aside our differences? Will I be able to submit to her rule? If only I live to try.

As a little girl, she had admired her mother, the power with which she ruled, the gentleness with which she judged, but later, as a young women, she had rebelled, wanting to do things her own way. Without the protection of a coven, she had been easy prey for Father Benedict and his hatred of all things female.

A chill shivered across her bare arms, where new burns smarted from Brother Adrian's torture. She touched them with tender fingers and whispered a spell. The pain ebbed, and the wounds stopped their festering. They would heal in a few days.

Poor Brother Adrian! Marissa felt only compassion for the mistreated monk. His soul, wounded more deeply than her body, cried out from pain and loneliness, once good and kind but now ruined to the core, one more sin on Father Benedict's conscience.

During her imprisonment, Marissa witnessed two burnings. She had reached out with her power to ease their pain and soothe their spirits and had almost lost her own sanity. She still heard their heart rending shrieks in her dreams. She wished she could have quickened their passing but she was not capable of destruction. Having witnessed their terrible end strengthened her determination to resist Brother Adrian's interrogations, although they became ever more painful.

The raven cawed again and settled her torn spirit. *I must have faith, help will come!* She heard one of her cell mates stir and hurried back to her sleeping place. Morning was near. It was Sunday. There would be no torture today.

"You have all received message that a great evil has been done," said Blessed Mother to the assembly. "All the signs have shown us that one of our own has been taken and that her end is near. We must now decide what to do. Should we expose ourselves and save her? Or should be let things take their course?"

Silence fell for several seconds before a hundred voices spoke at once.

"We cannot stand against the Church."

"How do we know it is one of us?"

"We must save her! What if it were you?"

"It is a risk we all take when we chose to practice the Craft."

And so on.

Blessed Mother raised her hand and hummed. The assembled Grand Coven fell silent. At that moment, a late arrival landed in the clearing, her broom falling sharply to the ground. A tall, slender woman of middle age leapt off the broom and looked around wild-eyed. Spotting Blessed Mother, she raced to her and flung herself at her feet.

"Do not let this happen, Blessed Mother! Do not let her perish, I beseech you. I could not stand it!"

A hundred pairs of eyes stared.

Blessed Mother reached down with soothing hands. "There, there, Elena. What has you so distraught?"

A sob escaped the woman, huddled on the ground. "It is my own daughter in the inquisition's grip. I did not know until today."

A low murmur swept through the assembly. How could she not have known?

"I see," said Blessed Mother, "You were estranged."

The woman nodded and wept. "Would that I could change that now. If we save her, I will let nothing come between us."

"Dry your tears, child. We will find a way. There is more at stake even than just your daughter's life."

"You will help me?"

Blessed Mother let her gaze sweep over the assembly and studied the faces of her charges. Some remained closed with angry eyes and furrowed brows, others showed kindness with tears glistening. The ancient one nodded.

"We will. And I will tell you all why we have to."

She beckoned to Thalia and Raynier who hurried to Elena, their Reverend Mother, helped her to her feet and led her to sit with their own coven. They did not leave her side.

"We have known for some time that one of our own was taken by the Church. After hundreds of women burned at the stake, falsely accused of witch craft, now they finally got their hands on a real witch. Her name is Marissa and she is the daughter of Reverend Mother of Shadow Coven. This, we did not know until today. Marissa has been questioned by the priests, tortured, and starved. She is near breaking. If she confesses, if her life ends at the stake, we will all perish.

"We could not save all those innocents who lost their lives but we must save this one. Vision upon vision has told me this. If we do not, our world will live forever in darkness and there will be no end to the killing, the maiming, and the madness. We have this one chance to turn the wheel of history. The stars are lined up; it is the right time to act, the only time to act. If we fail, the world will end in bloodshed. If we succeed, a new age begins and we will all move toward a brighter future.

"We will light fires and burn sacred herbs and we will dance and chant to raise energy. We will work spells of healing and enlightenment and we will find a way. We cannot let our world perish. It is up to us to save it."

From each coven came one to draw a brand from the center fire. Each coven lit its own hearth. Some raised a cauldron above it, others sprinkled herbs right onto the flames. Before long, thick smoke rolled through the clearing, reeking of burnt plants and setting minds afloat on its magic. The witches began to chant. They twirled, they writhed, they stomped, they leapt. Men and women held hands and vaulted over fires. Capes swept the ground and fluttered through night air, hair flew, eyes blazed. Even Blessed Mother danced, and none danced more ardently than Elena. Magic swirled in a vortex and soared toward the heavens, dimming the stars. A light broke from the center of the vortex, and sparks rained on the assembly.

After a while, the voices became quieter, and the movements gentler. The rain turned from fire to water and drenched out the fires, all but one, the tall blaze in the center. Blessed Mother stood beside it, alone, with tears streaming from her eyes.

"I have the answer," she cried out. "I have the answer but it breaks my heart to tell you."

A hundred witches crowded around her, offering support, questions in their eyes.

"What is it, Blessed Mother? Can we save Marissa?"

Slowly, the crone nodded, and she seemed even more aged than before.

"We can but it will require a sacrifice."

"What must we sacrifice?"

"It's not a what, it's a who. One of us must walk into the fire, and another must follow to change the world. It is the only way."

Elena pushed through the crowd.

"I will do it. She is my daughter. I will gladly die for her."

But the old crone shook her head. "You cannot. You must be there for your daughter to heal the rift between you. And you must give your love to those who will sacrifice."

She turned to the others. "One who loves her most will step forward but it cannot be her mother."

A long silence followed. Witches looked at the ground, at the stars, at the fire, but not at each other, not at the mother and not at the crone.

"I will," said a small voice and Thalia stepped forward. "I love her like a sister, and I will give my life for her and for the world."

The old one nodded but before she could say anything, a man's voice cried out. "No! You cannot leave me. I will not let you."

Thalia turned her head toward Raynier, brows furrowed. "I am not your wife. You cannot forbid me anything!"

But Raynier stepped to her side and grasped her hands. "All these years, I have waited. We will have a future together. I have loved you so long I have forgotten there was ever a time when I didn't. You are the bravest of all witches but I can't let you go."

Thalia took his hand, kissed it, and laid it against her cheek. "Dearest Ray, if only you had said something. All this time, we could have been happy."

"I thought we were. I thought you wanted distance."

Thalia smiled a sad little smile. "No woman wants distance. Not even when she is a witch."

"So you'll not do this? You'll take my promise and be mine?"

She shook her head. "Don't you see that I cannot? I have to save the world."

Raynier sighed. For several minutes, he just held on to her hands without speaking. Then, he kissed her lightly on the lips and said, "Wherever you go, I'll go. We will save the world together."

They came for her again in the morning and led her to the torture chamber in chains. She could not stop her heart from racing, or her breath from catching in her throat. When they tied her to the post, she wept. Brother Adrian had the forge going, and his irons glowed in the blaze. The monks had removed her cotton shift, and she shivered, despite the heat.

Marissa wailed from fear. Her skin glistened from sudden perspiration. She lost control of her bladder.

"Please," she sobbed. "Please don't do this again. I have nothing to tell you."

Brother Adrian hummed. He took one of his hot irons and pressed it to her bare leg. She screamed. Her shrieks should have crumbled stone, but the walls stood, and Brother Adrian calmly returned the iron to the forge. Marissa howled. She whimpered. She nearly choked on her own tears. Brother Adrian picked up another iron.

No one knew how it happened. Perhaps Brother Adrian felt faint from lack of food, perhaps he took a wrong step, but he stumbled with iron in hand, cried out and fell into the forge face-first.

He leapt back roaring, hands reaching toward singed flesh. He fell to his knees and moaned. "Help me!" he cried, reaching for Marissa and turned his ruined, now blind eyes toward her. The fire had wrecked his gaunt face, licked down his neck and scorched his shoulders. Only his apron had stopped the flames from ravaging his trunk. Marissa cried out when she saw skin fall off in patches. His shrieks reminded her of the women burned at the stake.

She knew better, but she spoke the spell without thought, so terrible was the sight. She spoke it three times, and when she was done, Brother Adrian's screams stopped. The angry red of his flesh paled, and his eyes cleared. He felt no pain but only wonder.

"How did you do that, witch? And why?"

Marissa dropped her head, sensing her own doom. There was no help for her now.

Later, back in the dungeon, she had time to weep while she listened for sounds from outside where they built her pyre. She would burn by morning. She wondered how long she would suffer. Brother Adrian walked the cloister halls with his brethren in sunshine. His belly no longer growled, he had been well fed. Yet in his soul lived sadness he could not explain.

The bonfire roared. No one had stoked it for hours, yet it had not consumed the wood. Elena stood with her arms around Thalia and Raynier and wept. Her heart throbbed with gratitude, guilt, love, and loss. The three held on to each other, giving and seeking support, trembling with the magnitude of what lay before them. Blessed Mother waited patiently by the fire, and the crowd stood in silence, heads bowed, eyes wet with tears.

"I should not let you go. I should be the one," sobbed Elena. "I cannot find words to thank you that will not bring me shame. I love you both so much, and our coven will honor your memory for ever. We will never be the same without you."

"Reverend Mother, it is good this way. Although I am saving the world, I am doing it for love of my friend, your daughter. Please tell her that my heart sings when I step into the flames. I do not want her to carry any guilt over my passing."

Raynier didn't speak. He had eyes only for his love, the bravest witch of all the covens.

"It is time," said the crone, and Elena stepped away, still crying.

The two young people embraced once more and waited until their trembling ceased.

"I love you, Ray," said Thalia. "I love you for loving me, for being my best friend, for not leaving me in this hour."

He nodded and smiled. Then, with arms wrapped tightly around each other, they stepped into the flames.

Flowers bloomed in the meadow outside the monastery. Their scent blew into the dungeon when the walls crumbled to dust. Three women stepped out of the shadows into sunlight, eyes wide with wonder. Chains dropped from hands and feet, and the women felt light as feathers. They danced through the meadow on bare feet chasing butterflies. Tears of joy glistened in their eyes, but only one of them understood what had happened. The witches had kept their word. They were free!

A raven alit on Marissa's shoulder and nuzzled her ear. She reached a tender hand to stroke his shiny black feathers. Behind her, the monks watched with benevolent smiles on their faces. A middle aged woman stepped out of the woods into the meadow, arms wide.

"Mother!" cried Marissa and threw herself into those arms, her heart skipping for joy.

"My darling daughter. You are safe, and the world is healed. Nothing else matters now."

"What happened?"

"There was a ritual. And a sacred sacrifice. But all is well now."

"A sacrifice? But who...?"

"Don't you worry, child. It is over."

"Who, mother? Who lost life because of me?"

Elena sighed. "Thalia and her friend Raynier. They said to tell you they saved the world but they did it for love of you."

"Saved the world? How so?"

"Look around you, daughter. Their sacrifice moved us from the Dark Age into Light. The universities will be teaching science, women will be free to marry or not marry, to own property, to go to school, and we will be free to practice our craft. Look at the flowers! They were not here this morning. The world rejoices."

Marissa's eyes grew sad. "Indeed it does, but my friends suffered on my behalf."

"I think not. When they stepped into the sacred fire, they did not cry out. They just vanished into the flames, and a great sphere of light shot into the sky, blinding us all with its brightness. When we could see again, two new stars twinkled in the heavens. Your friends will live for eternity."

"Mother, I want to come home."

"Of course, dear. The coven welcomes you."

"The coven...what about you?"

"You are always welcome, my darling."

"We have lost so much time, Mother."

"Yes we have. And now we will make the most of what we have left in this age of enlightenment."

The Dance Fairy

On the last day of school, Todd asked Sarah to marry him. His proposal came out of the blue and threw the whole town into uproar. And when she said 'yes,' tongues didn't stop wagging for months. The two hadn't even been dating, had they? Nobody in their right mind would date Sarah.

Anyone could tell, Sarah was part Fae. Her olive skin tone, overly large green eyes, and high forehead gave her away. And of course, there were those oddly shaped ears, not long and pointed like a full Fae, just unusually slender, delicate, and almost transparent. No one knew where she came from when she moved into town with her human mother, but rumors abounded. Some said, her mother was raped by one of the Fair Folk, others insisted she had made herself a harlot and got stuck with a half-breed child.

When Sarah entered high school, she was shunned like a pariah. She sat by herself in the lunch room and put up with daily hassles like racial slurs, having her books knocked on the floor, and finding disgusting things stuffed into her locker. Sarah bore these insults without complaining. Her shy, gentle nature never changed. Her tormentors never let up either, and Todd was one of the worst. So why, on the last day of school, did he pop the question?

They didn't know that Todd had secretly been peeping in Sarah's window and was overtaken with desire for her willowy body and the grace with which she moved. They also didn't know that Sarah had been taking ballroom dancing lessons from a private tutor, and that Todd burned with jealousy every time the tutor touched her slender waist. So people figured she must have put a spell on Todd, had him hexed some way, and they tried their best to talk him out of his mad proposal or pray him out of it. Nothing worked.

Reality looked a bit different. Todd had offered Sarah a ride in his pickup that day, and she refused, not trusting his motives, so he followed her, driving slowly and calling out to her through the rolled down window.

"You really should consider marrying me. I have a decent job, and you don't have a lot of options."

Sarah stopped and stared. For a moment, she looked other-worldly, as though her Fae blood was pulsing more strongly through her veins.

"Say…what?"

"Well, you're out of school, you don't have the money or the smarts to go to college, and they won't hire you down at the bean plant. Way I see it, I'm your best bet."

"But…but I thought you hated me!"

"Nah, I just had to put up a front to make it through high school. Besides it was kind of fun, messing with you."

"It wasn't any fun for me."

"Oh come on! Don't be like this. High school is over, and you have to think about your future. Do you want to live with your mom the rest of your life and be an old maid?"

"I'm only seventeen."

"And I'm eighteen. We're just right for each other. And I don't mind that you're half-blood. I think we could make some pretty babies."

Sarah blushed and dropped her gaze. She wasn't used to being thought of in that way. She cast a look at him through her lashes. He was good-looking in a rough cast way. What he lacked in charm, he made up with shapely muscle. Most of the girls had dated him at one time or other. Except Sarah.

"I would have to think about it."

"Well, think about it then. I'll come by your house tomorrow morning. And every day after that until you say 'yes.' I mean, seriously, what else are you going to do with yourself?"

Sarah's mother flew off the handle when she got the news.

"After all he's put you through, he wants to go and propose? What kind of joke is this? Must be a bet or something."

"I don't know mother. I just know he asked. He'll be by tomorrow."

Todd did show up the next morning and recited his unromantic proposal in front of Sarah's mother.

"I make good money. She won't have to worry about working in the bean plant or cleaning other people's houses. Just mine."

"But, why my Sarah? None of you have ever been nice to her, least of all you."

"I'm aiming to change that. Once she's married to me, nobody will mess with her."

"I just have a hard time believing you. This is some kind of trick or something to give my Sarah a hard time."

"No trick. I'll prove it to you. I'll go get my dad."

Nobody knows what the adults haggled out but Todd and Sarah sat outside and tried to have a sensible conversation.

"You don't love me."

"You don't know that, Sarah. I'm just not one who uses that word."

"What word?"

"You know...the 'L' word."

"From what I hear, you said it plenty to Susie Carter."

"Sarah, that was in fifth grade. That doesn't count. I didn't even know what that meant then."

"And now you do?"

"Well, I'm willing to find out."

He bent to kiss her, strong lips on her soft ones and Sarah, who had never been kissed before, felt tingles in her toes.

The wedding was a small affair, only parents and Todd's siblings invited but when they stepped out of the church, a crowd of gawkers had assembled. Nobody spoke. They just stared.

Sarah wore a pale blue dress and looked ethereal, and Todd drew every girl's eye, dressed in a white shirt and dark blue suit. They made quite a pair. Todd's siblings had decorated the pickup, and the young couple took off on their honeymoon, dragging tin cans and a pair of old boots.

They didn't get far. The pickup caught a flat, and Sarah sat in the cab listening to Todd cuss and throw wrenches. After a while, he stuck his head in the window.

"I can't get the damn thing off. We're gonna have to walk."

Hours later, hand in hand, they arrived at the cabin Todd's father had given them. The wedding night which followed was a disaster. Todd, who used to play football, knew how to score a touchdown but didn't waste his energy

160

on subtleness. Sarah, a virgin, wept and bled and wept and bled. The sheets turned crimson, and her skin faded to gray. In a panic, Todd called his parents on the cabin phone. They, in turn, called the ambulance.

Sarah spent her honeymoon in a hospital bed with Todd sitting sullenly at her bedside. He blamed himself, and then he didn't. How could he have known that she had an odd blood vessel too big to clot? He didn't blame Sarah either. He just resented her. He had turned his back on his friends for her and for what?

Despite the bumpy start and despite the gloomy prediction of the town folk, once Sarah came home from the hospital, their marriage settled into a harmonious normalcy. Todd went to work, and Sarah kept house and tended the garden. She read and sang and practiced her ballroom dancing, now without her teacher, and when Todd came home, she served him a good meal. Over time, though, their romance-less intimacy made Sarah wilt like a flower.

Years passed, and no babies came. Doctors called Sarah a hybrid and pronounced her barren, and Todd brooded. He was still smitten with her but he saw his dreams falter. Sarah slipped into a deep sadness.

Todd began to frequent the town pub, and sometimes Sarah went with him, especially on Wednesday nights when the band played ballroom tunes. One night, she tried to get Todd to lead her to the dance floor but he refused.

"I don't dance."

"You could learn. It's not that hard. I'll show you."

"I'm not going up there to make a fool of myself. Nobody else is dancing."

"We could practice at home."

Todd's fist came down on the table, hard. "Goddammit, I said no!"

Sarah shrank from him, feeling his anger like fire on her fairy skin. She slipped from her stool and ran out the door into the night.

"Go after her, man," said the bartender, but Todd shook his head. He wanted to drink, not comfort a crying wife. In the corner, he spotted Susie Carter, still single, with two of her girlfriends. He raised his glass. She smiled. No drama, that's what he needed. When Sarah returned, his arm was around Susie's shoulder.

Sarah's eyes went wide, and her knees buckled. She might have gone to the floor but a strong arm caught her, and a warm baritone voice murmured in her ear, "Steady now, steady. Let's get you out of this stuffy place into some fresh air."

She turned to look at the speaker through a veil of tears with his arm still solid around her shoulders and barely stifled a cry. Forest green eyes burned into hers with a depth and fire she had not seen since her father died. Long, pointed ears swiveled toward her like cats' ears. The stranger's face was of an olive hue darker than her own. Others in the pub might not have deemed him handsome, but Sarah, whose Fae blood called out to her own kind, fell into those eyes, instantly smitten.

"I'm alright now, thank you," said Sarah and felt with wonder that she really was. His arm around her felt a dozen times warmer than a human arm and ignited her chilled heart. She leaned against him, marveling at his scent, which reminded her of forests and sunshine and deep, dark earth. And then he kissed her, and her world spun with stars of vivid colors.

"What the hell?"

A male voice she vaguely recognized shattered her bliss. Reluctantly, Sarah's gaze tore away from the stranger to settle on her husband whose eyes blazed under a forehead grooved with anger, and whose arm still draped over Susie Carter's shoulders. Sarah smiled, noting the irony even though her belly cramped with fear. She need not have worried though because the stranger stepped between them, one hand raised and said only one word in a quiet, baritone voice.

"No!"

Though it was quietly spoken, that one word seemed to roll out from his tongue, spill over the crowd and splash up the walls of the pub. Everyone stopped to listen. All eyes turned to watch. Todd's arm fell off Susie Carter to his side, and he backed away. The only sound in the pub was the music.

The stranger took Sarah's hand and led her to the dance floor. She followed him, light-footed and graceful. He snapped his fingers, and the music changed, the melody and beat familiar but the instrumentation different from any she had ever heard. He placed his arm around her slender waist, and then they danced.

It was nothing like the lessons she had taken, although the steps seemed the same. They moved as though they had danced together for eons. Sarah's willowy form became possibly even more willowy, her lithe movements even lovelier.

"You dance like a queen," said the stranger and pulled her closer. Sarah smiled, and a light came into her eyes, spilled out and swirled around them. It rose in hues of blue and emerald green, licked across the ceiling and dripped onto the Wednesday night crowd. Shadows quivered and retreated into the walls. Lamps and mirrors began to gleam with that same, eerie light, the liquid in the glasses sparkled. People stared, and Sarah and the stranger kept on dancing.

A scent of moss and clean water went up from the girl and mixed with the aroma of earth and forest trees, coming from the stranger. Under the lovely smell, Fairy pheromones rolled off the pair and tickled the noses of the gawkers. And suddenly, all the young men who had once done her so wrong wanted her, hard with desire, hearts beating like drums. And the women who sensed the change in their husbands and lovers felt their own hearts ache with jealousy. And still, Sarah and the stranger danced.

"We Fae have magic when we dance. Did you know that?" murmured the stranger.

"We do? What kind of magic"

"Whatever kind we want. There is much power in a fairy dance."

"The power to heal? To hurt? Or to make people love us?"

"All of it and much more but only when we dance."

"I would want them to love me, even for just a little while."

"They already do. See how they yearn!"

Sarah turned her head and wherever her gaze fell, a young man dropped to his knees or a woman bowed her head and cried. She spotted her husband, awash in adoration with eyes only for her, Susie Carter abandoned in the corner.

"Come," she said. And Todd fell at her feet and wept. Sarah and the stranger kept on dancing.

"What else would you want, lovely Sarah? Name your desire."

"I would want him to be sorry for what he did to me."

"He is. See for yourself."

Todd cried out to her, blaming himself for all their troubles, promising to be the best of all husbands, if only she would forgive, forget. Sarah smiled, and Todd wept with love for her.

"Is there not something more you want, my fairy queen?" murmured the stranger, his warm lips close to her ear, his hot, sweet fairy breath making her shiver. The light in her eyes darkened, and her lips tightened. Her dance steps grew harder, less flowing.

"I would have them all pay for the pain they caused me."

The stranger smiled and nodded. The music changed, and he led Sarah into a faster dance. More men knelt. More women wept. And then Sarah turned to look at them, green eyes ablaze with fury, and all who met her gaze began to bleed from eyes, ears, noses and from their very skin. Screams filled the night as the town folk fell, writhing in agony and regret, knowing it was too late to repent, their doom imminent. She almost let Todd live for the years they'd had together, for the kindness he had shown her by marrying her. Almost. But she remembered all the evil he had done before and the coldness after, and her heart hardened.

"You must pay for being wicked, Todd," she whispered. "Just like everyone else."

"No, Sarah, wife! You said you'd forgive me. You took my promise."

"Your promise won't last, Todd. I only have this moment."

"I swear it to you by all that is holy."

For a moment, she hesitated. Todd noticed her uncertainty, and his eyes lit up. He reached for her, and she took his hand and quickly dropped it, his touch all too human, his fire too cold. The stranger pulled Sarah close and held her, Fae body to Fae body, matching his steps to hers.

"He is not for you," he whispered. "He will chill you to the bone."

"Yes," said Sarah, and she turned again to Todd, death blazing from fiery eyes.

He screamed and fell into fetal position, clutching his belly and rocking from side to side. Blood oozed from every pore, his cries weakened, and his pulse slowed to nothing as he spilled his life at her feet. She watched it fade without remorse, smiled even a little, power holding her in its terrible grip. They all died in the pub, and when they no longer moved or cried, the music stopped, and the stranger let go of Sarah's hand. Heart pounding and breath racing, she took in the carnage around her.

"What have I done?"

The stranger smiled and his smile no longer felt warm but chilled her.

"You met your darkness."

Sarah fell to her knees and sobbed, cradling her dead husband in her arms. "Look what you made me do!"

The stranger shook his head, ears now laid back against his head and brow furrowed.

"This is not my doing."

"But I loved him. I love him still."

"You do not. You are Fae. You cannot love a human. It is against nature."

"I am *half* Fae. My mother was human. She loved my father."

"Your father – where is he now?"

"He died. Years ago. But he loved us both."

"He died – and so will you if you stay with these humans. We would have kept you, raised you but for your mother who snatched you from us. It took all my cunning and magic to find you."

He reached for her, but she shook her head, his charm no longer affecting her. Revulsion ghosted across her Fae features, and she shrank from him. The stranger sighed, sadness in his eyes. He held out his hand over Sarah, and the air began to swirl. From his palm a green light flashed and washed over Sarah and the bodies beside her. She cried out and began to keen, rocking on her heels and hugging her arms to her chest. He waited one more minute, hoping for her to call out, to reach for him, to choose her Fae kin but she didn't. She stayed huddled to her dead husband's form, hate and grief in her eyes. He snapped his fingers once, and green light flared brightly, and Sarah, the half-breed sank lifeless to the floor. The stranger sighed, stepped over the bodies and walked out the door, tears in his forest green eyes.

A Day Without Magic

One October morning, Tabitha's wand didn't light the fire under the cauldron. She tried several times, to no avail and thought maybe the wand had gotten wet. She put it away, carefully avoiding any damp areas and brought out her spare. She spoke the spell out loud this time, something she rarely did and only when the spell was new or very complicated, and pointed her spare wand at the black, cold coals. Nothing! After several attempts, brow creased with frustration and hand shaking from growing fear, when the wand didn't tease out so much as a spark, she ran to wake her sister.

"Shonda, something happened to my magic. I can't seem to raise a spell!"

Shonda, dark haired, dark eyed, and bronze skinned, the opposite of Tabitha whose blonde hair fell in tight ringlets onto fair skin, and whose blue eyes blazed, stretched and blinked in confusion.

"Tab, you know I'm not a morning person. Can you keep it down?"

"My magic, Shonda! I think I lost it."

"What are you talking about?"

"I can't raise a damn spell. I can't even strike fire."

"Well, that's odd," said Shonda, the queen of understatements.

"It's a disaster! I have five potions to make just this morning, and I am supposed to bless the fields this afternoon and do a demonstration at the college at five this evening."

"What did I tell you about taking on all that extra curricular stuff?"

"Well, one of us has to do some public relations work so they don't start coming after us with pitch forks, and you don't seem to volunteer."

"People don't use pitch forks anymore, Tabitha."

"Whatever. Guns are no better. Especially when I don't have magic to turn bullets aside. Now can you get up and help me?"

Shonda sighed. She resented busy bodies so early in the day. She flipped back the covers and sat up. She picked up a brush and began to brush her long, straight black hair, letting it fall over shapely bronze curves. She always slept in the nude.

"We don't have time for this. Put some clothes on and come help me!"

"Okay, okay, give me a minute!"

Shonda slipped into a silk gown without bothering with underwear and picked up her wand. She pointed it at her bed like she did every morning to straighten the sheets and covers and spoke a word. Nothing happened.

The sisters looked at each other with growing unease. For about a minute, neither spoke, their breathing the only sound in the room, and then both of them cried out at once, "The unicorns!"

They raced from the room, down the stairs, and out the front door. Barefoot with hair flying, they scampered across dew-wet grass to the stables where two mares with their foals lay listless in the straw, eyes shut and breath labored. The sisters knelt beside them, looking them over, examining with keen eyes and gentle hands.

"They're sick. They may be dying. Someone blocked our magic. How could this happen? And who would do something like that?"

"Tab, I don't know. Who would want to hurt a unicorn?"

"Do you think our potions still work?"

Shonda shook her head. "I don't know but we have to try."

They opened a cabinet and took out several flasks of different shapes and sizes. Shonda scratched her head.

"We could try the purple elixir. It fights weakness and lack of appetite."

"And maybe rose oil with butterfly dust?"

"Yes, that may help balance their chakras."

"Dose the foals first. They seem to be fading faster."

They opened equine mouths and dosed according to weight, then massaged the unicorns' throats to encourage swallowing. Lacking the ability to cast healing spells, they prayed – to the gods and goddesses, to the elements, to the spirits of the sun and moon. But the sun was busy rising and the moon busy setting, the gods and goddesses were not listening, and the elements remained silent. The unicorns' breathing grew shallower, and their eyes didn't open.

Tabitha lept to her feet. "I have an idea. I'll be right back."

She ran to the house and returned shortly thereafter with an old, leather-bound tome of considerable size and weight. She slammed it on the stone floor and began to leaf through it with increasing speed. Shonda watched without comment. Suddenly, Tabitha stopped and cried out in triumph.

"Here it is! This book is as old as the hills but it has what we need. A healing potion that needs no magic to cure the loss of magic."

"That's extraordinary."

"It's a miracle! That's what it is. We just need to gather the ingredients and brew the potion."

"Well, let's hear it. What are they?"

Tabitha shoved the book over to her sister and they both bent over the yellowed parchment page. Shonda whistled through her teeth.

"Where in all blazes are we supposed to get monkey breath?"

"Or porcupine quills? Or the paw print of a male lion?"

"Are you sure this book is legit? It's not a joke or a child's toy?"

Tabitha nodded, her face grim. "I'm positive. It cost me a small fortune, and I trust my source. I better be able to trust my source!"

"Well, let's get started then. We can get the plants pretty easily, and then there is the zoo…"

An hour later, the two sisters hovered by the monkey cage, tossing banana pieces through the bars. At first, the little primates stayed back, reaching with long arms for the food, eyes fixed on the humans outside their enclosure, but after a while, their caution lessened, and they scampered to the wire for more. With hands, feet, and prehensile tails grasping the bars, they hung suspended and poked noses through the wire, screeching with greed. Shonda had the bottles ready and captured several puffs of monkey breath before tossing the rest of the bananas into the cage.

Quills were trickier but Tabitha climbed the barrier and leapt over the trench into porcupine habitat, wearing thick leather gloves. For several minutes, she chased one of the rattling animals around the rocks before she got hold of it. She let go immediately, cursing in every language she knew. Several quills stayed stuck in her gloves, and they had gone deep. She pulled them out and tossed the gloves, her hands bleeding.

"Your turn," she said without even a trace of a smile.

The lion cage presented a problem. Not only were several visitors huddled in front of the habitat but the enclosure was made of glass and the big guy inside didn't seem in a friendly mood. He paced and roared, his manly bellows amplified by the speaker system. Shonda tiptoed and peeked around the spectators. The ground was wet, and the big cat had left several clearly visible foot prints. If only they could get inside and do so without being eaten. Shonda shuddered. A knot formed in the pit of her stomach. Then, she raised her head, pulled her shoulders back and took off toward the back of the building.

"Where are you going? Wait for me!"

But Shonda shook her head. She needed no witnesses. She knocked on the door to the lion keeper's office and entered without waiting for a reply. A lanky, middle aged man with sparse, slightly oily hair and a five o'clock shadow looked up from his computer and stared. A grin crept over his ungainly features, and he leaned back in his chair.

"Well if it isn't the sexiest witch in Jackson County. What brings you to my humble abode?"

"Hello Mac. How are you today?"

"Getting better now that you're here Shonda. What can I do for you?"

"Well, I need a favor."

Mac's grin widened. "You don't say."

"It's really important."

"How important is it, oh lovely one?"

"Well, it's a matter of life and death, really."

"Ah, that kind of favor, huh? That might cost you."

She wanted to turn him into a frog. Or a rat. But his answer didn't surprise her. There are few surprises for a witch – besides losing one's magic. She suppressed a shudder and pushed her violent thoughts back where they had come from. There was always time for such things later, after the unicorns were safe.

"Name your price."

He did not answer but held his hand out, hooked his fingers and beckoned her to him. She closed her eyes and swallowed. When she opened them, she was all vamp, all seductress. She glided to the desk, put her arms around his neck, and sat in his lap.

She pressed her forehead against his, looked him deep in the eyes and said, "I need two minutes in the lion's den – without the lion."

"OK, but you'll have to do more than just sit there."

She straddled him. His hands slid along her supple curves and he buried his face between her ample breasts, breathing her scent in deeply. She moved a little against him and felt him harden. And what followed after that was for nobody's eyes and ears and for Shonda to bury for ever in the deepest, darkest recesses of her soul.

She lifted the lion print with a knife and placed it carefully into a small cardboard box. She left without looking back, though Mac stood by the habitat with admiring eyes. Tabitha waited outside full of questions.

"Don't ask. I have the damn print. Let's get out of here."

They prepared the remedy with the utmost of care, boiled it down to a syrup and poured it into small, shallow dishes to cool. One teaspoon every hour for the foals, three for the mares. Now all they could do was hope and wait.

Meanwhile, a group of farmers stood by a cotton field grumbling, and no witch came to bless it. A few folks had come knocking on the empty house, looking for potions. A man died for lack of magic and then another. But the town people had a different interpretation. By evening, guns came out of cabinets, and the town square echoed from heavy farmers' boots. College students slipped on their hoodies and grabbed baseball bats. Everyone was in agreement: The witches were not playing by the rules. Something was going on, and the sisters would have to answer for it.

By sunset, the unicorns had recovered some of their strength but they still had a long way to go. The sisters looked like they'd been fighting a war. Neither had eaten anything. Tabitha's stomach threatened to cave in and Shonda sat on the ground, rubbing her tired feet. They decided to sleep in the stable with the unicorns, afraid of leaving them alone. They had just huddled in the straw when they saw a flicker of light through the cracks in the wall. Tabitha peeked out the window.

"There's a damn posse out there. They're headed to the house."

"No kidding?"

"Shonda, why would I be kidding about this? I'm telling you, there's a damn posse out there. I'd say at least fifty flashlights and a couple of torches."

"Oh they wouldn't! Would they?"

The sisters clasped hands in the dark and fell silent. Fear so cold and dark it took their breath away rose between them. Fifty or more angry towners were paying them a visit, and they had no magic to fight them.

"If they catch the house on fire, we'll lose everything," whispered Tabitha. "My wand…I know it's useless, but I still should have taken it with me. I've had it since I was thirteen."

"My books," murmured Shonda. "I can't lose my books." She leapt to her feet and would have run out of the stable, if Tabitha hadn't grasped her ankles and tripped her. Shonda sprawled on the stone floor, cursing.

"Shonda, for crying out loud. They have guns."

The sisters sat in the dark, panting, waiting for the inevitable to happen, watching the angry towners advance on their house. Baseball bats struck against fence posts as college students psyched themselves up for destruction. Farmers cocked their shotguns. The sisters heard glass shatter and the ring of metal on metal. The smell of burning tar wafted toward the stable.

And just when their lives were about to go up in flames, when everything they had worked for was about to be destroyed, one of the unicorns nickered, and Shonda felt something burn a hole in her pocket. She cried out and with a look of wonder and utmost relief pulled out her old wand and held it high. Its tip was aglow, and it vibrated, very much alive.

"It's back! The magic, it's back," she cried, pulling her sister to her feet. "Let's go stop this madness!"

She walked with her wand held before her, lighting the way, Tabitha close behind, speaking incantations. There was a rush of air, and the torches went out. Then, the metal in the guns began to heat and glow. The farmers dropped them, shouting obscenities and shaking their burned hands to cool them. Baseball bats turned to powder and fell at the feet of hooded youths. A shout went up among the crowd, and they turned and ran, tripping each other in the scramble to get away. In less than five minutes not a soul remained.

A loud whinny came from the stable, and four unicorns trotted out, tossing their silver manes and stomping their alabaster hooves. Shonda and Tabitha wept with joy.

They packed their most prized belongings and hitched the mares to the wagon. Shonda had to leave some of her lesser books behind, and they took only small vials of the most precious potions. They destroyed the house with a blast of light and seeded the place with grass and flowers. By sunrise the next morning, they were gone, and nothing was left to show that witches had ever lived there.

The Elephant

Things had become strained between the witch and the mortal when he brought the elephant home. Natasha clapped her spell book shut when she saw them and gaped.

"Gregory, what in the name of all things magical is that?"

"It is a thing magical."

"I can tell that. I can smell his signature from here. I can smell other things too. I thought elephants were clean creatures."

"He's a bull. They have an odor. It is part of his power."

"Well, can you get him out of here? He's too large for this little house."

"He's here for me. He'll stay and defend my space."

"Defend? Against what? Or whom?"

"I need my own space. This is *your* house, *your* land, *your* furniture, *your* space."

"But honey, when we married, everything I own became yours too."

"Yes but it was yours first."

She shook her head to clear it. Confusion showed on her face.

"And what is the elephant going to do for you?"

He will square off my space whenever I need it. He will change things to my liking. He will stop you if you intrude."

"You would put an elephant between us?"

"Not just any elephant. He's magical."

"I know he is. How does this make things better?"

"He will stop you if you get too close."

Natasha watched the pachyderm close in around her husband in a tight circle while keeping her in sight.

"We're married. I'm supposed to get close."

"I need more space, and I don't like that you hold so much power."

"I'm a witch. I can't help that I have power. But it's not about the power."

"Easy for you to say. You're a witch."

She shook her head vehemently, and her braids flew. Her eyes darkened with passion. How could she make him understand?

"Marriage is not about that. It's not about how to have more power or more space. It's about sharing. Anything that comes between us is not good. It hampers the flow of love. It hampers the sharing. We have enough between us as it is, more than most couples. Don't you see that?"

He started to say something. She could tell by his eyes, he wasn't listening, not deeply with his heart. "But…" he began.

"No! There is no 'but.' If it comes between us, it is a bad thing. Please, do not do this." She paused and studied his closed face for a second. "Unless you're done," she said more quietly. "You could be doing all this because you're done. Are you done?"

He thought for several long, empty seconds and nodded. "Yes."

"Well then, get out,' she snapped and her voice turned arctic. "Pack your shit and get out. I never want to see you again."

The elephant raised its trunk toward her and trumpeted. It stamped its feet. It swished its tail. She backed against the wall and raised a forbidding hand.

"Don't you dare come any closer, beast!"

The elephant sucked air until it inflated to twice its size. Then it blew all that air and a considerable amount of snot in her face so hard it knocked her off her feet. She screamed. She slapped her hand against the floor and swore. The ground rocked, and the elephant squealed. Its eyes rolled, and its trunk grasped wildly for a hold but found nothing strong enough to stop its fall. It smacked down hard on a hip and slammed its trunk down in anger. The mortal hid behind the furniture. The very same furniture he had disdained only moments ago.

Natasha leapt to her feet and faced the downed animal. She raised her hands and began to stroke the air. It looked like her hands were dancing, and the pachyderm's eyes followed her movements, mesmerized. Gregory crept from behind the furniture to watch. After a while, the elephant's trunk waved in unison with her gestures, first twirling and undulating snakelike but soon moving with more purpose, writing symbols in the air while Natasha murmured incantations. Still lying on its side, the elephant sighed deeply, laid its great head down, closed its eyes and fell into a deep sleep.

"You hateful witch, you stole my only source of power!"

"So I did." Natasha's voice could have chilled the fires of hell. In her eyes blazed a cold blue light. Her hands still danced but silently now. She stepped forward into the space once protected by the now sleeping beast. "Now we will know the whole truth, won't we?"

Gregory clenched his jaw and resolved to say nothing but after a moment, he began to moan.

"Who is she, and what have you done?"

Gregory fought against the compelling force but without much success. Word by word, she pulled the truth from him, scorched him dry of all his evil doings. First, the name of the mistress, then her whereabouts. Then, the plans of binding the witch, of escaping together with Natasha's money, riding the magical elephant into the sunset. The whole ugly story poured out of his unwilling mouth and spilled at the witch's feet.

Natasha smiled a bitter smile. She spoke a word, and the elephant awakened and rose. It plucked Gregory off his feet with its trunk and slung him over its shoulder against the wall where he slid down and landed with a dull 'thud.' He shrieked, and the pachyderm swiveled around and eyed him coldly. Gregory cursed.

"Get over here beside me! You were mine first. Don't you dare side with the witch."

The elephant swayed, swinging its trunk. It didn't move from its spot.

"You filthy beast! You will not defy me!"

Gregory snatched up a chair and slammed it against the elephant's head, tearing its ear. Blood trickled. The beast raised its trunk and trumpeted. It plucked the chair from Gregory's hands and smashed it to bits. It turned its intelligent gaze on Natasha who stood with arms crossed, watching the confrontation. She shrugged.

"He's all yours. I'm done with him. Knock yourself out."

At once, the elephant reared and trumpeted. It came down hard on its forelegs, felling the mortal and breaking his back. Natasha heard bones snap. The elephant trampled him to mush, then picked him up by his hair and slammed him against the wall, over and over, until Natasha raised a hand and stopped it.

"We have work to do," she said and climbed on the animal's trunk and from there over its head to its back. "Let's go visit the mistress."

The Cloud Catcher

She leaps over rainbows to catch clouds.

She has a way of bunching them together, like cotton stuffed in a quilt. With nimble hands, she shapes them into towers, castles, and foreign beasts. It is her only talent, and no one knows how hard she works at it. She has been zapped many times when static builds and lightning leaps from cloud to cloud, turret to turret. Lightning has frizzed her hair and singed her skin to a rich bronze. She has no eyebrows. Her left eye is blind, cooked by an angry sun: She came too close once. She turns her head slightly sideways when she looks at you. It does not deter from her charm.

She lives on the kindness of friends, surfing from couch to couch, eating at a different table each day. She does not go to work like other folks but when the mist blows in, fogging away the stars, she leaps tirelessly and works harder than any.

You and I lie on the grass, hand in hand and stare at the clouds. We watch how she shapes them and guess their final form.

"It's a dragon. No.. It's a dinosaur."

"But look, now it's different. I think it's a mammoth."

We do this every Saturday, rain or shine. In winter, we huddle under blankets.

She always gives us something new to admire. And when we tire of guessing, we make love under open sky, and she is kind enough not to look.

I never realized how lonely she was until she met Durk. He charmed his way into her life and for a while, the clouds hung fat and shapeless from the heavens. Durk wooed the Cloud Catcher with dogged persistence. Her shy nature caused her to stutter in his presence, and she almost fell from the sky one day when he called her name. She wrapped herself in his affections, slipped into them as one would a warm winter coat. She mimicked his manner of speech and was baptized into his faith. She drank up his bewitching words and beamed, giving the clouds a rosy glow. She was lonely no more.

Until Durk ran off with a Gypsy girl.

Now her mind stays on the clouds. She builds bigger castles with taller towers. Her beasts are more foreign each time. She never smiles, and when she weeps, the rain turns salty. She is the kindest person I know with a most charitable heart. Everyone loves her. Everyone steps off the path to help her, yet she seems sad. From time to time, she still turns the clouds red. That's when I know she's thinking of Durk and his wicked charm.

Night Hunter

He slinks from tree to tree, shadow to shadow. Moon ray plays over his golden form. His fur glistens. He creeps with nose on trail and scents. She went this way not long ago; she can not be far. Pricked ears catch a rustle in nearby bushes. Can he have found her?

He loves her by day, but now he feels only hunger. He salivates at the thought of her rich, dark blood and tender young flesh. He drops to his haunches under the branch of a giant pine. Wind carries a familiar scent to his flared nostrils. Is it she? It has to be.

Only hours ago, he caressed her body, loved her moist depths, but now his chops drip with anticipation. The wolf in him almost howls.

He rises and trots toward the sweet fragrance. He will have her. It will not be long now.

They met only weeks ago, and already she is under his skin, her scent and voice sweet torment to him. He found her in a meadow, resting from picking berries in nearby woods. Dark hair swept up into a pony tail revealing her delicate features, she looked up at him without surprise, as though she expected his sudden appearance. He had followed her scent with flared nostrils - human nostrils - and when he stood over her, blond hair falling to his shoulders, blue eyes agleam with laughter, she smiled and patted the ground beside her. And later, when he kissed her, the ardor with which she kissed him back surprised him.

He seeks her now, nose high and nostrils wide. He does not know what he will do without her tomorrow, but tonight he is hungry. Why is she out walking in the moon light? She should have stayed home where she is safe from him in this changed form.

In the meadow, a girl waits. The moon reflects in her eyes and caresses her alabaster skin. She knows, her lover is near; she always does. She feels him because the air changes when he moves. Tonight, the air is warmer than usual, and she knows, he, too, is seeking the full moon, is drawn to restlessness by it. She smiles, and pheromones roll from her body and scent the air with sweetness. She is ready for him.

He bounds from the trees toward her, tongue lolling and eyes sharp. He can taste her now. Yet, when he leaps to pounce on her, to bury his teeth in her throat, to rip with giant canines, he feels the ground shake. She changes before his eyes. Dark fur pops out where only moments ago smooth skin beckoned. From her hands, claws grow, hook-like and sharp. Legs angle into powerful haunches, and her face, oh her lovely face…!

He falls short in his leap and lands hard, eye to eye with the biggest, shaggiest she-wolf, he's ever seen. Her snout reveals fangs, strong enough to rip him to shreds, but her manner is friendly. He throws back his head and howls, and she does likewise. They sniff each other for a long minute, reading intentions in each other's scent. Then, they trot away, side by side to frolic under the full moon, hunger momentarily forgotten.

The Deed of Old Reya

Old Reya didn't understand why the boy was given a unicorn to ride. He was about the last person, she would have let near a unicorn. His father, Lord Robert didn't let him ride his prized thoroughbreds, and young Edward about ruined his own little Welsh pony with spurs and a most severe bit, riding rough and hard. Old Reya snuck into the stables when she could to put the healing to the old pony, but she had no power to stop the abuse, and when she encountered the boy somewhere on the trail or in town, she bowed and scraped like the rest of them.

The young viscount had been clamoring for a new ride, claimed, he'd outgrown the sturdy Welsh, complained, it was undignified for the son of an earl to sit lower than the guard. So for his fourteenth birthday, Lord Robert, Earl of Bright's Castle bought his cruel son a unicorn. Old Reya watched from the shadows as the splendid beast danced into the courtyard, hitched to the back of a wagon. She was a gray filly with a fine, glossy coat, a silver mane and tail, small, delicate hooves that sparkled in sunshine, large, intelligent eyes, and a short, blunted horn which seemed to emit its own muted light. She was too young for riding, yet, there she was, her noble head in a high curb bit, clearly too severe for any young horse, especially a unicorn.

Young Lord Edward glowed with pleasure when his father handed him the reins. "Now that's more like it," he exclaimed and tugged on the rein sharply, promptly causing the filly to rear and toss her head. Edward grinned, and a dangerous light came into his eyes. He reached to his waist, where a riding crop dangled, raised the crop and brought it down sharply on the filly's neck. The unicorn veered to the side, and Edward followed, whipping her around the head and neck with speed and fury, while pulling the filly's head down, down, down.

"You *will* learn to mind me, you wild nag. I have a few teaching tools I'll introduce you to."

"Edward," Lord Robert snapped. "For crying out loud. That's no way to treat a fine filly."

"She's mine, father. Didn't you say so? I need to break her to my will. Her blood is too hot. I aim to cool it a bit."

"There are other, better ways to do this."

"Well, my way is faster. I've waited long enough for this mount. I don't plan to wait all summer to ride her."

Robert shrugged. "Don't come crying to me if you ruin the filly. She's not as sturdy as that Welsh."

But Edward didn't hear him anymore. He was already trotting the unicorn to the training pen, tapping her with the crop every few strides. The unicorn danced and snorted eyes wide with fear.

Old Reya had stepped out of the shadows when the whipping began. She stood, frozen, wanting to help, wanting to run and hide, unable to do either. She stared, eyes burning, as the viscount hooked the filly to a long line and picked up the big whip. Edward spotted her over the fence.

"What are you doing here, you old witch? Trying to hex my horse? Get out before I have you tied to the stake!" He raised the whip and cracked it in the crone's direction.

She's not a horse! thought Old Reya but she said nothing, only scuttled back into the shadows, heart pounding with anguish.

The viscount lunged the unicorn for an hour or more, smartly popping her haunches with the tip of the whip. He knew his business. Had he been a less cruel man, he might have been a great horse trainer. He lunged her one way and then the other until foam flew from the filly's mouth, and she stopped running, stood, shaking, lathered in sweat. He laughed, tugged on the rope, and the filly came to him, wary, but obedient.

"There, that's better. Don't anyone have to tell me how to break a nag."

He swung a blanket onto the filly's back and heaved a saddle on top. The filly stood, trembling. He cinched the saddle girth tightly. The unicorn did not move He adjusted the stirrups and led her to a stand where he tied her. Then, he climbed the ladder and plopped on her back, snapping the reins loose. The filly almost went to her knees. He kicked a spur into her side, and she bucked. Edward held on and drove the filly forward. She raced along the fence, looking for a way out, sparks flying from her hooves. A high-pitched whinny tore from her throat. She danced. She bucked, she ran. Until her lungs gave out, and she stood, head hanging low, the light in her horn dimming. And Edward threw his head back and laughed.

Old Reya crept into the stable that night, herb satchel and salve in gnarled hands. When she saw the filly in her ragged state, she almost wept. No food or water had been left for the tired beast. Dried sweat still clung to her coat, and she breathed heavily, her nostrils flared.

"There, there," she murmured. "Let Old Reya take care of you."

She hauled water from the fountain, buckets full and tossed a flake of hay into the stall. The unicorn heaved to her feet, snorting. While she drank, the crone checked her injuries: a few cuts from the whip and swollen tendons on all four legs. Old Reya treated the cuts with poultice and rubbed a stinking salve into the unicorn's legs, murmuring spells while she worked. After a while, the filly's breathing eased, and she buried her nose in sweet smelling hay. Later, they lay together on the stall floor, the crone resting her head on the filly's back. They slept until just before sunrise, and then Old Reya sneaked back out.

Over the next few days, the same scenario played out in Lord Robert's training pen. The viscount ran the filly almost to death before getting on her back. Each time, she bucked a little less, remembering the pain of the punishment. Each day, the light in her horn dimmed a little more. Old Reya came to the stall every night with her healing potions and spells. She eased the filly's pain and restored her strength, but she could do nothing about the light in her horn. And Old Reya grew as despondent as the beast she tried to protect.

The day came, when the light was almost gone, and the unicorn's magic almost extinguished. She trotted like an old mare, offering no resistance. Her head hung low unless Edward brought it up, hands on the reins, tugging on the bit in her mouth. Old Reya in the shadows wept with helpless fury, and when she looked through the veil of tears, she thought the unicorn, too, was weeping. That was the moment Old Reya remembered her calling.

That night, she freed the filly, walked her right out of the stable, quietly, across the courtyard, behind the well house and off into the field beyond. She walked until she couldn't walk anymore, and then she spoke a gentle word, and the unicorn knelt to let her mount. Old Reya rode ever westward, out of the earl's estate, through the silent woods, and into the wilderness, leaving behind everything she knew and everyone she loved. She cared not about her own safety, wanted only to be far away when dawn cracked, when, surely, Edward and the earl's guard would be looking for a unicorn and an old witch.

There was uproar at Bright's Castle. For weeks, all anyone talked about was the escape of the gray filly and the disappearance of the crone. No one ever heard of either one of them getting caught, and as far as anyone can tell, they either perished in the wild or reached some kind of safe destination, living happily ever after.

Cold Maid

When Ta'Shaun woke up, she found herself, body and tail, frozen to an iceberg. She tried to pull away, but she was stuck so solidly that tearing away would rip off more than just a few scales but would lay open half of her body and mortally wound her. She lay still for a while and tried to remember how she got in this predicament.

She had partied hard with the Mermen and injected herself several times with blowfish venom to get high. One of the Mermen had found a particularly powerful blowfish, and they had milked it dry, but it wasn't until she shocked herself with the eel that she lost consciousness. She didn't remember anything after that.

With her small hands, she checked herself over for injuries. Her skin was intact, both on the fish tail and the humanoid body, except for the tracks of blowfish injections. There were no broken bones that she could tell, although she could not move her tail. She ached all over, probably aftereffects of the electric shock, and when sharp pains shot through her lower half, she realized, the Mermen had violated her.

Had she spawned? She had no memory of it. Perhaps tiny Merkidlids were already floating in the deep sea with her blood flowing through them. She wished, she would have been mentally present for her first spawning. She wished, she had been able to choose the day and the Merman.

Overwhelmed, Ta'Shaun wept large, salty tears. She had no idea where she was adrift on her iceberg, how far from her cozy home among the anemones. She missed her sisters who had warned her not to trust the Mermen. She shivered in the cold, dry wind.

After a while, her skin began to crave moisture. She could just dip her left hand in the waves and splash herself but not enough to keep from dehydration. If she stayed here much longer, she would surely die. She wrung her delicate hands and sobbed.

In her misery, she did not hear the dip-dip of kayak paddles or the sharp intake of breath when two young adventurers' eyes fell upon her lovely face and shapely body. But then a deep male voice said words, she didn't understand in a language she had never heard before. Her eyes flew open, and she dropped her hands and gasped.

"Well, would you look at that," said Danny, his voice barely above whisper. "It's a frozen Mermaid."

Danny and Ron found a place to pull their kayaks onto the ice and secured them with ropes and spikes, which they drove deeply into the ice. They clambered onto the ice, pulling themselves up with picks and stood panting over the strange creature, scratching their beards. She had frozen deeply into the ice until it cradled her body. Long, greenish-brown tresses flowed from her head, surrounding a face with deep-set eyes the color of the sea. Her small-lipped mouth opened and closed, fish-like. A set of gills sprouted behind shell-shaped ears. Her skin had a gray hue with no pigment flaws or body hair. From her hips down, gray-green scales hugged a powerful fish tail. She flailed webbed hands at them, the only parts of her body that remained free. Her eyes widened when the humans towered over her, and she keened softly, fear crawling like crabs up and down her back. The men squatted immediately and her fear ebbed.

"There, there, we are not going to hurt you," murmured Danny with a voice that would soothe the most feral of beasts. He looked up at Ron. "Now what?"

"I guess we'll have to get her off the ice berg somehow."

They broke the ice with picks, careful not to get too near her. They loosened her from her prison with buckets of sea water, melting the ice a little at a time. Though they were careful, some of her skin tore and some of her scales stayed on the ice. It took most of the day to free her. By sunset, they heaved her into one of the kayaks and paddled to their cabin, a good two miles away. She lay in the kayak without moving, eyes closed, and only the rise and fall of her chest let them know she was still living.

"We have to get her into water, Ron. I know that much."

"Does it have to be salt water though?"

"Hang on, I'm checking." Danny snapped open his laptop and searched.

"It can be half and half. They sometimes swim up a river, and they do just fine."

"Alright, lets get a few buckets full and then fill the tank the rest of the way with melted snow."

They hauled many buckets of seawater from their kayak landing site to the cabin, slowly filling the tank. They had pulled the kayak across the snow to the cabin, and the Mermaid still lay in it without moving or opening her eyes.

"She's heavy. It's going to take both of us. Let's just lift her from the boat and dump her in."

"Seems wrong but what choice do we have?"

They plopped her into the tank where she submerged with a surprised cry. But the tank was shallow, and she hit bottom and came up thrashing and flopping her tail. She hissed and showed small, pointed teeth.

"I think she's a predator, and I bet she's hungry."

Ron tossed a small fish into the tank, and she dove for it, brought it up to her face and sniffed it. Then, she dropped it back into the water and huddled in the corner of the tank, eyes darting from Ron to Danny and back to Ron.

"Maybe she only eats live food?"

Danny sighed. He fished out a live squid from the aquarium and dropped it into the tank. The Mermaid snatched it up and devoured it. Then, she rolled over on her back and floated. Her tongue darted in and out of her mouth and made clicking sounds. The men looked at each other and shrugged.

They sat up late into the night, surfing the web for information and watching the Mermaid sleep in the tank, submerged now, breathing through her gills like any other fish.

"Danny," said Danny, pointing to himself. "D a n n y."

The Mermaid sat squashed in the farthest corner of the tank and stared.

"I know you can talk. I heard you yesterday. and I've read all about your kind."

Again he said his name and pointed to himself.

"Ehwy?" asked the Mermaid.

"Danny."

"Tanny?"

"Close enough." He nodded, smiled and pointed at her.

"Ta'Shaun," said the Mermaid.

"Ron, she's a quick learner. Her name is Ta'Shaun. I told you she could talk!"

"I heard her. But you're a long way from finding out where she came from."

"Do you think she could understand a map?"

"Not unless it has underwater views. She's not a bird, Danny."

Ta'Shaun detached herself from the corner and floated to the center of the tank, looking at Danny with large, sea-blue eyes. "Tanny!"

Danny pointed at himself again. "Man. I am a man."

"Maan."

"You are a Mermaid."

"Mrr-mait?"

For a while, they continued, naming body parts and objects in the room. Ta'Shaun repeated to the best of her ability, eager to learn. She scooted ever closer to the edge of the tank and suddenly reached out a webbed hand and placed it on Danny's arm. He shivered. She jerked her hand back and placed it on her own skin. Then, she pointed at the fire and at the snow outside. Danny nodded.

"I'm warm. You are cold."

Indeed, it had felt like a fish touching him in its coldness, but, although startling, he found it not unpleasant. He laid a hand on her arm. Her eyes widened.

"Warm."

Ron found them later, holding hands, gazing into each others eyes. He sighed.

"You know you can't keep her."

"Ron, leave it alone. I'm doing research."

"On a *Mermaid*?"

"She's a marine species, isn't she?" Danny's voice rose in anger and Ta'Shaun backed away from him, frowning.

"Easy, there, easy. No worries. I won't hurt you," purred Danny and Ron shook his head and walked away.

Ta'Shaun woke late in the night. The stars had already given way to a shroud of fog, and the only light in the room came from the glow of still hot coals in the fireplace. After a minute, her eyes adjusted, growing larger and darker to accommodate for the lack of light. She was jonesing for some blowfish venom. She wasn't hungry. Danny had fed her well, but how would she explain to him that she needed a fix? He was so gentle. She recalled the heat of his hands on her skin and shuddered with pleasure. She knew he liked her, wanted her, but he had not made a move. Why could not the Mermen have been so respectful? She lay back in the water and sank to the bottom of the tank where she slept on the hard floor, wishing for sand and seaweed.

"Can Mermaids have sex?" asked Ron the next morning, when Danny fed Ta'Shaun a fish. "Because you seem like you're headed that way."

Danny blushed. "Ron, shut up. You're embarrassing her."

"She doesn't even know what I'm talking about, but you...you're as red as a tomato."

"Goddammit, Ron! Are you jealous?"

"Why would I be jealous? I don't like women without nipples."

The breast-like protrusions on Ta'Shaun's chest, though shapely, did indeed have no nipples and, although mostly covered by the Mermaid's long, green tresses, occasionally peeked through, giving the men an idea of Ta'Shaun's sensuous anatomy.

"Why would she need nipples? She doesn't have to suckle her young."

Ron laughed. "So she is - essentially - a fish."

Danny leapt to his feet. "You're an asshole!"

Ron stepped back, hands raised in supplication. "OK, OK, I'm sorry. I didn't realize you were so smitten. I just meant, I'm not jealous, just - worried. About you. I've read too many tales of men falling for Mermaids and loosing their heads."

Ta'Shaun watched the men argue, not knowing what it was about. She reached out to Danny and laid cold hands on his bare arms, watching chill bumps rise on his skin. How intriguing! No Merman had ever shown such response. He turned and smiled at her and she smiled back, and he hurried to her side. She was craving venom again and tried to convey her need, but he didn't understand. When he noticed her trembling, he put his arms around her and rocked her gently, and it felt like the sway of the ocean.

Ron was right, Danny was smitten and he didn't really know why. He had never even dated out of his own race and Ta'Shaun was an entirely different species. He became accustomed to the chill of her skin, as she did to his warmth. And one day, she invited him into the tank. He stripped out of his jeans and joined her, still in boxer shorts.

She tugged on the boxers, curious, and he slipped out of them, breath tight and waited, trying to still the guilt in his mind and the fear of her. She dove and looked him over, moving around him, getting really close to his sex, and he worried, remembering her sharp teeth. But then she slithered up beside him, wet and beautiful, her hands cool and gentle on his man parts, and he took her in his arms and kissed her. She tasted like fresh air and sea water. There was nothing fishy about that kiss. He held her with utmost tenderness, and she showed him her opening and guided him in.

It wasn't easy. He didn't fit well, but they managed, and when they found their way together, their rhythm, it was bliss. Ta'Shaun thought of the Mermen, and how she would have liked Danny to be her first. Afterward, he rocked her again until his lips turned blue from the cold water.

"Tanny," she said. "Tanny." Just that, but it made him smile.

"You can stay here with me," Danny said, pleading with his eyes. "I have no need to return to the city."

Ta'Shaun had lived in the tank for two months, and her eyes sometimes got a faraway look. She loved Danny, with a love as strong as the rolling sea. Every day, she invited him into the tank, and every day he joined her. Some days, they just talked and held each other, some days they mated. Ta'Shaun had tried to spawn after copulation but none of her offspring lived. Danny's seed was not strong enough for a Mermaid. As much as she loved him, sadness crept into her eyes and voice, knowing that if she stayed with him, she would never spawn. She did not answer.

She missed the sea. The tank was never quite briny enough. Danny tried but his skin didn't crave salt. She missed the waves and her bed of seaweed, but most of all she missed her family and the wide expanse of the ocean depths, hunting for food in a coral reef, flitting through the waves hand in hand with her sisters. She no longer missed blowfish. Her blood ran clean.

"Tanny, my man," she said but shook her head. His eyes darkened.

In the nights, she sang softly to herself, of love and sacrifice, of loss and letting go. Sometimes, she would see herself with the man she loved, living forever in this cabin. Other times, she felt the walls cave in on her, and she dove to the bottom of the tank to breathe water. Some days, she wanted to rage at this human who had cleaved her heart in two and gave her such pain and such pleasure.

Another month had passed. Ta'Shaun was losing weight. Danny worked twice as hard to catch fish to feed her. She ate to please him but with little appetite. Her eyes, when they followed him around the cabin, were sad. Her skin had long since healed, and her scales re-grown. There was no physical reason for her slow fading.

Their love making had become even more passionate. Afterward, she clung to him and sometimes wept against his shoulder. Ron, who had mostly left them alone, began watching her intently and with furrowed brow. One day he approached his friend.

"You can't keep her against her will. She's a sentient. It's unethical."

Danny's head spun, and he leveled a glare at Ron. "What makes you think she wants to leave?"

"Look at her! She's homesick. She's just a shadow of what she used to be."

"Oh now, suddenly you care? She would tell me if she were unhappy."

"No, Danny. She would not. She loves you too much."

Ron squatted at the edge of the tank and beckoned Ta'Shaun closer. She stopped two feet away and watched him warily.

"I know you love Danny. But if he went away, where would you want to be?"

Ta'Shaun studied the man for a while, trying to spy his intent. She understood the words but also picked up an undertone she had not heard in Ron's voice before: sincerity, caring, gentleness. She pointed to the window, to the door, then made motions with her hands, simulating ocean waves. She saw him nod. She saw understanding in his eyes. She looked from him to Danny and saw anger.

"Tanny," she said. "Ta'Shaun go home."

Danny's face fell and he turned away, hiding his pain in rounded shoulders.

"Go then," he snapped, and she wept, tears more salty than the water in her tank.

They carried her to the kayak landing site the next morning. Danny had his arms around her when they lowered her into the frigid water. They had told her to go south after she recognized certain fishes and underwater plants on the Internet, flora and fauna indigenous to her home. She kissed Danny one more time and promised to visit him, before she slipped out of his embrace and dove into the waves. Salt bit into her skin and made her

feel awake and alive. She sucked sea water
through her mouth and pushed it out through
her gills, savoring the taste of fish and
brine. With a mighty stroke of tail, she sped
away, never looking back at the human who
knelt on the bank and wept from loss and
longing.